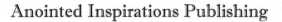

W9-BJM-067

Anointed Inspirations Publishing

Presents

Null and Void

A novel by

Tresser Henderson

DISCARDED

ALL RIGHTS RESERVED. No part of this publication may be reproduced, distributed or transmitted in any form or by any means, including photocopying, recording, or other electronic or mechanical methods, without the prior written permission of the publisher, except in the case of brief quotations embodied in critical reviews and certain other noncommercial uses permitted by copyright law. For more information, please contact the publisher.

Copyright © 2017 Tresser Henderson
Published by Anointed Inspirations Publishing, LLC

Note: This is a work of fiction. Names, characters, places and incidents either are products of the author's imagination or are used fictitiously. Any resemblance to actual events or locales or persons, living or dead, is entirely coincidental

Anointed Inspirations Publishing is currently accepting Urban Christian Fiction, Inspirational Romance, and Young Adult fiction submissions. For consideration please send manuscripts to info@anointedinspirationspublishing.com

Prologue

Amelia

How could my life be turned upside in the blink of an eye? I knew things like death, for instance, was unexpected and uncontrollable but at least I understood it because this was the time God was calling this person home. No one could argue with God on something like that. But this, this situation right here, right now, was pure devastation. I watched in horror as the police dragged my husband out of our home. They were arresting him and treating him like a common criminal. And who called the press. Why were they circling like vultures trying to find out why my husband was arrested? I was still trying to wrap my mind around it. Was he being set up? Was this staged? Did they have the wrong man, and this was a case of mistaken identity. What was this and when was someone going to say a mistake was being made. Regardless, this event was going to be documented and possibly televised to every news stations all over our city.

My brother, Diego, came into my master bedroom and told me the car was outside ready to take us to the station and that our attorney was going to meet us there. I sat on the side of my bed swiping at the tears that kept trickling down my face. My brother came over to the bed and sat next to me. Wrapping his arm around my shoulder he said, "It's going to be okay, Amelia. This storm too shall pass."

"Are you sure about that?"

"Just as sure as I know we serve the same God. He will never leave nor forsake us. You must trust in him. I know this is hard, but you will get through this."

I nodded, continuing to swipe away at my tears. I knew my immaculate make-up was ruined.

"You ready to go?" he asked gently.

Nodding I said, "Let me freshen up a bit and I'll be right down."

My brother smiled lovingly before he got up and left me to myself. I sat for a few more minutes wishing I could crawl in this bed and pretend like none of this was happening. Things had spun out of control. My chest began to tighten. My breathing became labored and I knew the stress of this situation was pushing me into a full-blown panic attack. I rushed over to my dresser opening the top drawer. I frantically began searching for my medicine and found the bottle of Xanax. Quickly opening it, I attempted to pour one pill in my hand, but my hands were shaking so bad, I ended up spilling half the bottle into the floor. Dropping to my knees, I picked one of the pills up and tossed it on my mouth. I swallowed it with no water hoping this feeling would subside quickly. As much as I liked to control the things around me, this was one event that was completely out of my hands and I knew the stress of not knowing what was going to happen was crippling to me.

When we exited my home, I covered my face as my brother escorted me to the SUV waiting to take us to the police station.

"Excuse us. Please, let us through," Diego told the many photographers and news reporters pushing microphones and cameras in our faces.

"Mrs. Reid, did you know about your husband's deceitful way?

"First Lady, how are your children dealing with all of this?"

"Mrs. Reid, are you going to divorce your husband?"

All of these were ligament questions I'd played out in my mind. Should I divorce Carson in his time of trouble? Did I know deep down my husband's dealings were not always up to par and I turned the other cheek because I enjoyed the comforts of our life? And what about Aden and Payton? This would devastate them both. I'd called them to come home as soon as possible knowing the news about what happened to their father would spread like wild fire, but I wasn't able to speak to either of them. As much as I was worried about their well-being, I had to get to my husband. I needed to speak to him and get a better understand of what was really going on.

"Please move out of the way," Diego demanded.

His voice was stern as he pushed one of the photographers out of the way who was blocking us from getting into the SUV. I could see my brother was getting angrier by the minute. None of these people cared about us. All they were trying to do was cover the next big thing which happened to be the destruction of my life right now.

Diego opened the door and I quickly entered the vehicle. He jumped in behind me, hurriedly closing the door. Lights were still flashing as the photographers tried to get more pictures even though the windows were too tinted for them to capture anything inside.

"Are you okay?" my brother asked as the driver proceeded to pull off.

I looked at him with a grief-stricken expression.

He reached over and grabbed my hand saying, "It's going to be okay, sis."

"Are you sure?" I asked with uncertainty.

"I'm positive."

"I'm not so sure this time, Diego. This is huge."

"True but nothing is too big for God. You should know that," he said.

"I know. I also know I need to give this over to the Lord. But as a wife, I have questions and need answers. I'm allowed to have doubt, right?" I questioned.

My brother nodded.

"I can't lie, I'm afraid. I'm hurt. I'm mad. I'm confused. All of these emotions are bubbling up in me and I don't know what to do with them, Diego."

"Just don't give up and don't give in to all this negativity. You are a very strong woman, one of the strongest women I know. I have no doubt you will get through this, just like you've gotten through all the other turmoil and tragedies of our lives. This is just another hiccup in life. And as soon as God quenches this situation, this hiccup will pass."

I gripped his hands as water welled up in my eyes again. I dabbed at the unfallen tears not wanting my make-up to be ruined yet again. I turned to gaze out of the window and watched the scenery as we made our way to the police station. I didn't know what was getting ready to happen but all I knew was my gut was telling me this was going to get a whole lot worse before it got better.

One Week Earlier

Amelia

The entire church stood when my husband approached the podium. There were claps of admiration, shouts of praise and music to elevate the true delight everyone felt now that my husband back where he belonged. I could tell he was getting emotional by the congregations applauds welcoming him back. With both hands planted firmly on the podium he held himself up as he pressed his lips together in gratitude. He quickly dabbed at the tears welling up in his eyes as the church continue to praise. I was so proud of him. He stood valiantly and looked handsome as ever. He was my six-foot four chocolate wonder. I knew I wasn't supposed to have lustful thoughts in church but at least it was for my very own husband. He was not only attractive, but he was sensual. The Lord knew my heart and knew I loved this man with everything in me. Even after being married to Carson for twenty-five years, I still loved him just as much, if not more, as the first time I laid eyes on him.

It was hard to believe we'd been together for this long. We'd been through so many struggles together but what marriage didn't have obstacles. I was happy we'd

9

made it thus far and trust me, we'd came a mighty long way. Carson being the pastor, and me, the first lady at the Greater Faith Baptist Church was a joy. We were the largest church in our area. I couldn't be prouder. So many said we couldn't do it or tried to hinder us from progressing forward, but God had a better plan for our lives. And despite all the nay Sayers, we did it with faith that God would get us through.

Thinking about how far we've come reminded me of a dream I had last night. I usually didn't dream unless the Lord was trying to tell me something. I wondered what the message was in that dream which unsettled me to no end. The dream felt so real. I woke up with my heart pounding and it took me a minute to figure out Carson hadn't been arrested. I even jumped out of bed and rushed over to the window to make sure news reporters and photographers weren't on our front lawn. I've searched my mind all morning and even prayed to God to show me what that dream meant. Was this a vision of what was to come? I prayed not because my faith within that dream was tested and it seemed as though I'd lost all faith in believing everything was going to be okay. I had to push that to the back of my mind right now and enjoy my husband returning to his rightful place in front of the church. I smiled as the congregation finally quieted down for Carson to speak.

"Let the church say Amen," Carson said.

"Amen," rang out.

"First and foremost, I always have to give God the honor and the glory," he said, pointing to the ceiling. "Because without him, I wouldn't be standing here today."

"Say it, pastor," someone shouted as the church erupted in more praises.

My husband grinned proudly, not able to say anything else as the church allowed the Holy Ghost to fill them. Even I got caught up in the moment. I danced in place, waving my silk lap scarf at the goodness of the Lord. Once the music stopped and the church calmed a bit, my husband continued.

"It's good to be in the house of the Lord one more time," my husband said.

"Yes, it is pastor," a member agreed.

"Please, y'all sit down, sit down," he motioned. "Y'all sure know how to make a man feel good," he chuckled.

"We missed you pastor," someone shouted.

"I missed y'all too. It's good to see all of you today. You know I was stricken with pneumonia for a few weeks and hadn't been able to preach but I'm thankful to be standing before you today."

"Amen," someone said.

"Me coming out of that sickness is just another testament on how good our God is."

"Amen" echoed throughout the church.

"I feel so much better. And I want to thank all of you who prayed for me and my family. Thank you for the get wells wishes, the cards, the flowers, and even food that was sent to us. I know my wife appreciated that because it saved her from having to cook," he chuckled.

"Praise God," I shouted with a smile as many laughed with us.

"Mother Betty sent me and my family an entire Sunday dinner last week that was more like a Thanksgiving feast," Carson said. "And I could have sworn my very own mother cooked it, may she rest in peace. The doctors wanted me to rest and as soon as I ate her delectable food, I was out like a light. Isn't that right honey?" he asked, looking at me and I nodded in agreement. This caused the church to erupt in laughter.

"You know what I'm talking about, when you eat food that's so good, it puts you to sleep. I always said the longer you sleep the better the food."

"Amen, pastor," many shouted.

"And as soon as I got back up, I was back in the kitchen for seconds."

More laughs echoed through the sanctuary.

"Thank you, Mother Betty," he said looking in her direction and she raised her hand smiling back at him.

"I know I've told you many times before but I'm going to tell the church here today. That woman over there is like a mother to me. She's prayed for me, fed me, lectured me, and even scolded me a time a two, ain't that right, Mother Betty?"

She nodded, waiving her handkerchief.

"She's been there for me during times I felt like I wasn't there for myself. Mother Betty is family to me. She's one of the most inspirational loving women ever and I love her dearly. Can you please stand up Mother Betty, so they can see your beautiful face?" my husband asked.

Mother Betty stood, waving joyfully at everyone. She truly looked younger than the eighty-two years she's been blessed with. She was a tiny woman but was stronger than anyone I knew. And she moved better than I did a lot of times.

"God might have taken my mother home, but God graciously gave me Mother Betty to play the role of a mother to me, my wife and our children, Amen."

"Amen," rang out.

As I sat in the third pew in the middle of the sanctuary wearing my light-yellow dress with matching hat, I looked over at Juliana who was waving her handkerchief in the air. She was rocking back and forth with her eyes fixated on my husband. From the way she was acting, you would have thought she was his wife and not me. I knew without a shadow of a doubt she wanted him. She'd already been through a portion of the men in this church. Why not go for the leader?

Please understand, I knew when my husband became a minister he would have many women throwing themselves at him. I was not naive to this fact. But it was something about this woman that got under my skin. She was like a bad rash that wouldn't go away. Being First Lady of this church, I had to carry myself in a respectable way. But trust, back in the day before I gained this title, I would have beat this woman down for even having the audacity to throw herself at my husband. But today and hopefully the days going forward, I knew I had to play this thing cool. I said hopefully because the street Amelia hadn't departed. She still resided within me. She was dormant now. But if this woman continued to push the limits thinking I was going to continue to grin and bear it, she would get introduced to a side I hadn't shown in a long time.

She must have felt me observing her. I was trying hard for my glance not to turn into a glare. Evidently it wasn't working because she glimpsed back at me smiling sheepishly. I felt like throwing one of these hymn books at her but returned a disdainful grin before turning my full attention back to the pulpit.

I saw my son stand and lift his hands for the choir to rise. They did so in unison. He looked over at the

Null and Void

piano player as the tunes to *Take me to the King* radiated throughout the place.

      I was a proud Mama. To see my son directing the choir and my daughter singing lead solo filled me with joy. It made me feel like I'd done something right in raising them. My son Aden looked so much like his father. I watched as Carson looked proudly at Aden waving his arms in the air as the choir's jubilant sounds uplifted each spirit in the place. And Payton, her voice was a true gift from God. She was giving Tamela Mann a run for her money singing this song. Many called her my mini me. I was happy to take that compliment because my daughter was a beautiful jewel.

      When Payton and the choir finished, most of the congregation was standing to their feet praising and clapping. Shouts rang out and I watched as my husband approach the podium since he too was already standing to his feet.

      Clapping his hands, Carson said, "Give the choir another round of applause. As usual they did a fantastic job, Amen."

      "Amen," everyone said.

      "And my baby. She gave me cold chills," she smiled at Payton. "Nothing warms my heart more than seeing my children uplifting God. I'm so proud of them."

I could see my husband was filled with joy and it done my heart good to see my husband back on his feet doing what he loved which was preaching the word of God.

"I'm here to give you all what you came here for today which is a word from the Lord. Please turn in your bibles to Romans 3:23 which begins *"For all have sinned and come short of the glory of God."*

Skye

I stood at the alter as Pastor Reid said a prayer for everyone within the sound of his voice. Tears streamed down my face as I whispered my own little prayer for my marriage. I wanted to wipe the tears away, but I was holding the hands of two ladies on each side of me. The one on the right was praising God and the one to my left was busy scolding the little boy standing in front of her asking her if it was over yet. He was so cute. He looked to be around three years old with chubby cheeks and huge curls like he should have been a girl. He noticed me glancing at him and quickly wrapped his arms around the woman's legs acting shy.

"That woman doesn't want you," she whispered to him. "She'd bring you back when she finds out how much of a tyrant you are."

He didn't look like a tyrant. He looked like a little boy being just that, a little boy. Little did this woman know I would give anything to have a child of my own. If I got pregnant today, it would make me the happiest woman in the world. However, my husband wasn't ready for that. The way things were going, I don't think he was ready for marriage either and this sadden me.

After church ended, I wanted to speak to Pastor and Mrs. Reid who were speaking to other members of the congregation. I waited patiently looking at Mrs. Reid and how beautiful of a woman she was. I knew she was in her fifties, but she could easily pass for her thirties. She didn't look her age. She was a fit woman with curves that turned a lot of the men's head in church. Despite their infatuation with her, Mrs. Reid only had eyes for her husband and I admired that.

With her skin a pecan complexion and her long tendrils of hair pulled up in a sleek top knot today, Mrs. Reid was the vision of class. She noticed me waiting to speak to her and instantly excused herself from conversing with one of the members to make her way to me.

"Hi Skye. How are you, sweetie?" she asked thoughtfully.

"I'm okay," I responded, thinking I shouldn't have said that since it was kind of a lie and here I was standing in God's house.

She noticed my uneasiness and asked, "Honey, you don't have to lie to me. I can see something is wrong. It's written all over your face."

I smiled awkwardly not saying anything because I felt like I could break down at any moment.

"Where is Seth? He didn't come with you today?"

That did it. That was all that needed to be said for the flood gates of my pain to spill from my eyes. Just like that, I broke.

"Honey," Mrs. Reid said taking me into her arms as she walked me away from everyone.

This is what I loved about her. She knew people were noisy. She always talked to me without an audience. Some ministers and their wives had things to prove but Mr. and Mrs. Reid were nothing like that. They were such kind individuals who I looked up to tremendously.

"Come on. Let's got to Carson's office and talk," she said walking to the front of the church. As we passed by offices and some of the clergy who spoke, Mrs. Reid smiled but never stopped her stride to get us to our destination.

Once we entered his office, she closed the door. She led me over to one of the burgundy leather chairs and sat in the one next to me.

"Honey, what's wrong? Is something going on between you and Seth?" she asked.

I nodded.

"Is that why he's not here with you today?"

I nodded again saying, "He's at home mad at me."

"What is he mad about?" she asked.

"I think he's cheating on me. I confronted him last night about it and of course he denied it. We had a huge argument that ended with him sleeping on the couch. He even told me if I didn't trust him, then maybe we should consider getting a divorce."

Mrs. Reid leaned back rocking a bit as she looked around. I could tell she was thinking. The lines in her forehead let me know this. Just when she was about to speak, Pastor Reid entered his office with one of the deacons behind him.

"Make sure you set that meeting up with the deacons for me," Pastor said to Deacon Dwight. When he saw us sitting in there, he cut his conversation short. "Okay Deacon, we will get together later to discuss this, okay."

The deacon nodded looking pass him to see Mrs. Reid with me in the office. Pastor Reid shook his hand before closing the door. He walked up behind me and placed his right hand on my back and asked, "Is everything okay?"

Mrs. Reid shook her head and more tears streamed down my cheeks. I swear it was like as soon as someone asked that question, it was the trigger that released them from me.

Pastor Reid walked around his mahogany desk and sat down in his large black leather chair.

"I take it this has to do with you and Seth?" he asked looking at me and then his wife.

Mrs. Reid reached over and took my hand into hers before responding.

"She thinks Seth is cheating on her and he's asked her for a divorce if she can't seem to trust him."

Pastor nodded as he asked, "Do you know for sure Seth is cheating?"

"A woman called and told me she was sleeping with him."

Pastor sighed before saying, "Well, that's huge."

"I don't know what to do. I don't believe in divorce. However, I don't believe in staying with a man that's going to do whatever he wants because he knows how I feel about the sanctity of marriage."

"I've known you for quite some time. I married the two of you and counseled the both of you before you decided to become one. You are a rare jewel, Skye. You have been in church most of your life. You have always respected yourself to the point you saved yourself for your husband. In today's time, that is rare."

"Yes, it is," Mrs. Reid agreed.

"I know when you said I do to Seth you wanted this to be forever. You took your vows seriously."

"I did," I responded.

""Skye, we can't tell you to leave or stay. I know you are not one to give up. As far as you have come and as much as you have accomplished, you know with God, you can get through anything, including this."

"I know," I said sniffling.

"Marriage is hard. Sometimes the only thing we can do at times is pray about it. Ask God for guidance. You know he will show you. Please understand, in God showing us, we don't always like what he reveals to us."

"That's so true," Mrs. Reid added.

"I love Seth so much. I still can't believe he had the audacity to mention divorce. I'm wondering did he say that, so he could get away from me to be with this other woman."

"Only he could answer that for you. You know I would be happy to speak with him."

"He won't do it. If he knows I'm speaking with the two of you, this will anger him more."

"I understand," he said.

"You two make it look so easy," I said.

"Trust me sweetie, this marriage has not been a cake walk. We weren't always saved and in the church like this. We were young and dumb and did a lot of stupid things to one another but through God's grace and our own determination, we made it," Mrs. Reid said.

"Yes indeed," Pastor added smiling at his wife. Things have happened that made us question whether we should have continued with this marriage also."

"But you worked it out."

"Only because we both wanted this marriage to work," Mrs. Reid said. "It takes two to make it work."

"That's my issue because it seems like I'm the only one who's trying to make this marriage work," I said.

"Seth seems like a good young man. Talk to him. Communication is key. At the same time go with your gut on how to proceed. The Lord didn't give us these instincts for nothing. You will eventually know what to do. And if you need anything from us, all you have to do is call," Pastor Reid said.

"Thank you so much. I just love you two so much. I appreciate everything you do for me."

Mrs. Reid leaned over and hugged me.

"Anytime sweetie. Anytime."

"I'm going to leave you two alone. I've taken up enough of your time," I said standing.

Both stood with me.

"We are serious. If you need to call us, we are here."

Mrs. Reid hugged me again before I exited the office. I wasn't sure what I was going to say to Seth when I got home but the one thing Pastor was right about was the fact we needed to talk.

Amelia

I knew I was a First Lady, but I was a woman first. I couldn't help but think about Skye and everything she was going through. I wanted so bad to tell her he was cheating on her. Any man that threatened divorce so easily had to be doing something outside of his marriage. I'd seen this scenario play out with many women. They love the man so much that they back off to maintain the sanctity of their marriage. Seth was playing games with her heart and her mind. He knew throwing divorce up in her face would cause Skye to shut down. He knew how serious she was about their marriage. For goodness sake, she saved herself for him. Even I couldn't do that for my husband. That alone should have proven to him how much she loved him. I wasn't sure what Skye was going to do but I would say a prayer for her and Seth.

It was time for Sunday dinner in the Reid household. This dinner would have been wonderful if Juliana Simmons didn't show up to our dinner table. And you knew who she had the nerve to show up with, my son Aden. They were linked arm and arm when they entered the dining room. I almost let the first lady image go out the window and cuss both of them out. How could Aden bring this woman in my house? He knew what type of woman she was. Then again, he knew what type of woman she was. This was probably why he was with her.

I tried my best not to roll my eyes at the two of them. It was bad enough I had to pretend I enjoyed being around my mooching sister-in-law, Delilah, who was now living with us. How did a couple of weeks equal to a few months? Can someone explain that one to me? If I knew this was going to be the outcome, I would have never agreed to allow her to stay. My home didn't feel like home to me anymore. It felt awkward with her being here acting like she was the lady of this establishment. I was so close to telling her just because she was blood didn't mean she was running anything around here because I was Carson's wife. I didn't know which was worse to have in my house, a whore or a leech.

"Mom and dad, you know Juliana. She's a member of our church," Aden introduced as he grinned from ear to ear.

"Hello Mr. and Mrs. Reid."

"Hello, Juliana. I saw you in church today. Did you enjoy the service?" Carson asked.

He saw her in church? Did he really need to say that? Was he watching for her like that? That's what it sounded like to me and I guarantee that's what it sounded like to her. Especially with the smile on her face showing all thirty-two teeth hanging out of her mouth.

Carson didn't know how close he was to getting popped upside the head.

"I did enjoy the service Pastor Reid. I'm happy you are doing better."

"Thank you. I appreciate that."

Was this really happening? All of them were talking like this woman being in this house was okay. She needed to go. I guess Aden saw the concerned expression on my face and decided to ask me about dinner.

"Mom, is dinner ready?"

"Almost."

That was all I could say as I glowered at the harlot who had her clutches on my only son.

She was determined to get her trifling behind in this family, whether it was gawking at my husband to seduce him or latching on to my son. She knew we had a prestigious reputation around this city and I knew that's what she was after. That and our money. I never imagined this woman stepping foot in our five thousand square foot home. But here she stood, bright eyed and bushy tailed. Goes to show it didn't matter if you lived in a gated community the enemy could still walk in through the front door with your family.

"Well, isn't she a pretty thing?" Delilah complimented looking Juliana up and down.

She probably was jealous since Delilah, who we also called Dee Dee, stood only 5'5" and looked like she was a size eighteen. She had the same chocolate complexion as her brother Carson and for a plus size woman could dress her behind off. But she was lazy as sin. She looked nice on Carson's dime, or should I say our dime. Of course, I was guessing but Juliana, even though I despised her, was a striking caramel skinned woman. She stood 5'6" looking like she weighed one hundred and forty pounds. Most of her weight was in her breast and behind. All her curves were on full display. Even though she was covered in a long sleeve red pants suit, the tightness of it didn't leave much to the imagination. And red? I know it could mean the blood of Jesus, strength and power but I knew in her case her suit was like a caution sign flashing danger ahead.

"Juliana, this is my Aunt Delilah," Aden introduced.

"You can call me Dee Dee. That's what everyone calls me."

"It's nice to meet you Dee Dee," Juliana said shaking my sister-in-law's hand.

"Girl, I needs me one of those suits. You are wearing that thing," Dee Dee admired with her uneducated antics.

"Thank you. I thought it might be too much for church but I took a chance anyway."

Took a chance in being seen, I thought.

"Well, you look marvelous."

"Thank you."

Carson could see the perturbed look on my face and decided to break up the camaraderie.

"Why don't we all make our way into the dining room?" he suggested.

As Carson began to lead them to the dining room, I kissed him. I also gave him a look of warning. He was married to me long enough to know neither her nor him better not step across a line that could get both of them hurt. I felt bad for thinking this way because Carson was not a man who stepped out on me, not that I knew of anyway. But there was always that chance or opportunity it could happen. Having the very woman who was willing to part her thick legs for most of the men sitting at the table didn't sit well with me.

Before my son could disappear with his uninvited guest, I called him.

"Aden, honey, can you come to the kitchen and help me bring the rest of the food out?" I asked.

"Sure," he said finally letting go of his side piece.

"I can help if you need it Mrs. Reid," Juliana offered.

"No…thank you," I struggled to say politely. "Aden can assist me all by himself. Please, have a seat at the table and we will be in there shortly."

"That's her way of saying she needs to talk to her son alone," Delilah said nudging Juliana.

I glared at Dee Dee only for her to smirk at me. There she went instigating again. She always like to stir the pot but was never there for the clean-up. Dee Dee was all talk but no fight. She could cut you down with her words and ruin people's lives with the gossip she told. But she would never fight with anyone. Now me, I was the opposite. I gave the smack down first and asked questions later. I'd changed, Lord knows I was trying, but if you came at me wrong, you could still catch these hands.

As soon as my son and I entered the kitchen, I lit into him.

"What do you think you are doing?" I asked with my hands on my hips.

"What?" he asked dumbly.

"How could you bring that woman in my house without consulting with me first?"

"Mom, come on. What's the big deal? She's a very nice woman. Besides, I knew you would have been against her coming."

"You got that right."

"You see, I knew it," Aden retorted.

"And since when have the two of you been friends of any sort."

"We've been talking for a minute."

"Talking like how?" I questioned.

"Talking mom. You know when two people's lips move, and words come out."

"Don't patronize me boy."

"I'm just saying," he chuckled.

"Are you with her because you think you can get into that tight suit of hers?"

"No!"

"I swear if it hugged her body any tighter, her face would turn blue."

"Mom, I knew you were going to do this."

"Do what?"

"Judge. She's really a nice woman."

"Nice? Boy please. There is a lot of nice young women in our church, but I haven't seen you bringing them to dinner. I know you. I gave birth to you and I know you are with her because you think you have a chance to sleep with her."

"Maybe," he admitted with a devious smirk.

"Boy, don't make me smack you. You know I have raised you better than that."

I turned away from him and drew in a deep breath calling Jesus in my mind. With a closed fist, I put it to my forehead. I could feel a headache coming on. And that was only because my blood pressure was rising.

"Mom, come on. Stop tripping. It's not that big of a deal. I'm a young vibrant man who happens to like sex. If I'm with a female who likes to have sex too, then it's all good for the both of us," he said shamelessly.

"You keep on. You are going to slide into something that's going to make your tally wacker fall off."

"Tally Wacker," he laughed. "I'm not five years old anymore. I'm a man. And if Juliana and I decide to take things further and my tally wacker happens to fall off, I'll deal with that repercussion."

"Boy, you are trying me today. Of all the women you could meet at church, you choose the one who's been with half the city. You could have chosen anyone but her. There is Susan and Nancy and even Sandra who are good Christian women you could have chosen."

"They are not my type, mom."

"So promiscuous women are you type?" I asked with frustration.

"Mom, Susan already has a boyfriend. Nancy is holding out for Mr. Right and Sandra wears bifocals and braces at the age of twenty-two. Seriously, look at me. Does it look like I should be seen with her?" he asked with his hands out posing and looking down at himself like he was the man.

"Aden, you are a very handsome young man, but you are letting these women blow your head up. You need to come down off that high horse of yours and humble yourself to a good woman."

"You mean settle down?" he asked.

"Why not? Your sister is, and she is younger than you."

"Here we go. Why are constantly comparing me and Payton. We are different people, Mama. I'm not ready to settle down. That's Payton's fantasy. She's dreamed of the white picket fence and kids for as long as I can remember. Me, that life isn't for me right now. I'm not saying I will never settle down, but I want to have fun for a while. Unfortunately, you are going to have to come to grips with that," he said sternly.

I noticed his mood change at the mention of his sister, Payton. His demeanor became somber and withdrawn and this bothered me. I didn't mean to compare the two of them, but it was hard not to at times. I hoped he didn't think I thought Payton was better than him because that was not what I was saying at all. I just wanted him to see that he was worth more than what he was reaching for. Aden was my wild child. I knew this about him. He had no fear about anything. He would be the one to jump from an airplane or bungee jump off a bridge. He didn't take things so seriously where Payton did. She was career oriented and knew exactly what she wanted. She wasn't a party girl and wasn't adventurist at all. Both of them were wonderful children. It amazed me how two diverse individuals could come from the same household.

"Honey, I'm sorry if I offended you in any way. I just want the best for you."

"I know mom. Please know you have done an excellent job as my mother. You are the best and I love you to death," he said with a warm smile.

"I love you too sweetie. And I will continue to mother you as long as God grants me breath to say what needs to be said, especially if I have concerns."

"I appreciate that. But please know your opinions may not change my actions. I'm a good man, mom. You've done a great job with me. I know I don't walk the straight and narrow like my sister, but I know right from wrong."

"Evidently not if you are with Juliana."

"Mom?" he said. "Here I am trying to be real with you and all you can think about is Juliana"

"Alright, Aden. I hear you. I just don't want to see you get caught up in any mess."

Aden approached me. He wrapped his arms around me. Of course, I returned the embrace. He was my only son and my first born.

"I love you, mom."

"I love you too, sweetie."

"Now, can we please eat because I'm hungry?" he asked.

"As soon as your sister gets here, we are going to eat."

No sooner than I said that, I heard the doorbell to our home and knew Payton had arrived.

Skye

When I got home from church and my meeting with Pastor and Mrs. Reid, I was disappointed to find Seth was nowhere to be found. I called out to him, which I found stupid since I didn't see his car in our garage. I guess deep down I was hoping he was here anyway. It did make me angry he couldn't go with me to church, but he could leave and go somewhere else without telling me.

I reached into my purse and pulled out my cell to see if he'd called me. There were no missed calls and no text messages. Going to my favorites, I chose Seth and dialed his cell.

"You have reached Seth. Please leave me a message and I will get back to you."

He'd turned his phone off. Why would he do that unless…unless? I shook my head hoping to shake the thought of him being with another woman out of my head but there was no use. Why else would he turn his phone off? What if an emergency happened and I needed to get in touch with him? Did he not take that into consideration?

I wanted to hear his voice. I wanted to talk to him, something we haven't manage to do in the past few weeks. We were just existing, not living. We were roommates, not husband and wife who loved each other. All because I accused him of sleeping around on me. How could I not when a woman called my phone to tell me she was sleeping with my husband. What? Was I supposed to hold that information and keep it to myself to spare his feelings? What about my feelings? As his wife, I had a right to question him, even though he felt like I shouldn't. My mother always told me if you wanted to know something, then ask and that's what I did. He screamed and yelled about it, of course denying it. He said I should trust him. I did, until I got that call.

Seth leaving without telling me his whereabouts and his phone going straight to voicemail was not going to help his cause. This further fueled my suspicion he was stepping out on me.

I kicked off my black stilettos and reached down to pick them up. I went to my bedroom to undress and get comfortable. Plopping down on the king size bed I looked around the room. It was so serene. With its muted blue walls, taupe drapery, cream colored throw pillows, and a crystal chandelier hanging over the upholstered taupe headboard, this room was a place of relaxation. I smiled at the space that we both compromised in. It wasn't masculine or too feminine. It was a mix of the two of us which I loved. This space was a complete contradiction of the friction we were having in our marriage.

Things weren't supposed to be like this. Not so early in our marriage. We were still supposed to be in our honeymoon stage but that was long gone. All because of that one phone call from a woman claiming to be sleeping with my husband. I contemplated calling the woman, not only to question her about what she told me but also to see if Seth was with her right now. And what if he was, then what? What was I going to do, ask to speak to him? Or was I going to get her address to roll up on the both of them. That would be the proof I needed to end things. But was this something I truly wanted?

I searched through my contacts until I came upon the woman's number. Ironically, I saved it under *the other woman*. I still didn't know what her name was and wasn't sure I wanted to know. Granted, I didn't think it was fair for this situation to be so one sided with her knowing who I was, but I wasn't ready to know that part of her. It was too much like admitting the truth. Until I saw for myself or heard Seth tell me he was cheating, I was finding it hard to believe. My gut was telling me different. My gut was saying something was going on with him.

Staring down at the number, my hand trembled as I contemplated calling her. My soul felt split in half with what to do and what to believe. If you would have asked me a year ago where I saw me and Seth's marriage, my answers definitely wouldn't have included adultery.

I hit the call button. The longer I waited, the more I would talk myself out of it. Nervously, I put my cell to my ear and listened as it rung. On the forth ring, someone picked up.

"Hello."

I didn't respond.

"Helloooo! Is someone there?" the female voice asked.

My stomach churned something fierce. My hand shook apprehensively as I opened my mouth and tried to say something, but no words would pass my lips.

"I'm going to hang up if you don't say anything," she warned.

"Don't," I blurted timidly.

"Who is this?"

"This is Skye, Seth's wife."

She got quiet for a few seconds before asking, "I knew you would call me back."

I said nothing.

"Are you looking for him?" she asked boldly.

Hesitantly, I said, "Yes. Is he there?"

"No," she answered.

A huge relief swept over me but only for a moment.

"He was though. He left about thirty minutes ago."

The core of my soul was sucker punched as my feelings of calm retracted to one of torment. She was talking to me like this was their norm, like he'll be home to you soon because I just finished up with him. The audacity of her. But how could I be upset with her. I wasn't married to her. I was married to Seth.

"He just left?" I asked for reassurance.

"Yes."

"What was he doing there?"

"Do you really want to know?" she asked recklessly.

I paused knowing whatever she told me could be another punch to my soul. Did I want to continue to torture myself with the details? My imagination had already conjured up what she was insinuating.

"Yes," I answered.

She giggled before saying, "He wanted to have sex."

"And did you?"

"Yes, twice as a matter of fact," she boldly stated. "He couldn't get enough of me."

40

Twice? Once was bad enough. What did this
woman have that I didn't? Seth had an able body wife in
me to unload his sexual desires on, but he had to go to
her. All he seemed to be unloading on me was his anger,
like I was the other woman, like I was the side piece. But
then again if I was his side piece, he would be treating
me better.

Feeling stupid for being nice to this woman who
claimed to be sleeping with my husband, I almost hung
up the phone. It was times like this I wished I had a
backbone to curse her out. I always let people walk all
over me. From the time I was a child, into my teenage
years. And now, when I was supposed to be an adult, I
felt weak just like the timid child I was. I hated myself
for being this way, for being so helpless.

"Are you still there?" the woman asked.

"Yes. I'm sorry I bothered you," I said wishing the
words that would flow pass my lips would be, you stupid
trick, how can you sleep with a man you know is
married. What type of woman are you? But those words
never parted my lips.

"Skye," she called out.

"Yes."

"I know what I'm saying to you has to hurt. I
debated telling you the truth but as a woman I felt like
you needed to know."

"Why would you sleep with him if you know he's married to me? Our last conversation, you were upset because you found out about me. So why would you still sleep with him. I'm confused," I said finding the strength from somewhere to ask her this.

"I'm with him for the same reason you are, Skye. You haven't left him either, after finding out about me."

"But I'm his wife. I love him," I replied.

"I love him too."

Love, I thought. *She's in love with my husband.*

"That's why I still deal with him. When it comes to matters of the heart, it's hard to relinquish someone you care so deeply for. I know what I'm doing is wrong but it's like I can't help myself."

"Do you consider yourself to be a home wrecker?" I asked.

"Yes," she said, surprising me with her answered.

The one thing about this woman she always seemed to amaze me with her answers. Deep down, everything she was telling me I felt to be true. She didn't hold anything back and was an open book about hers.

Hearing the beep of the alarm system let me know Seth was walking through the door.

"Do you think you can meet me for breakfast in the morning?" I asked.

"Sure. What time would you like to meet?"

"Is seven too early? I have to be at work at eight."

"That's fine. I'm an early riser."

After rambling off the restaurant located near my job we were going to eat at, I quickly hung up before Seth came traipsing in the room. I wouldn't confront him on his cheating and the fact I'd spoken to his side piece. I was going to play it cool for now. Until I had definite proof, I'd leave things the way they were.

Juliana

This family sure knew how to eat. Mrs. Reid threw down in the kitchen. Who knew she was such a great cook. I manage to smile and pretend like I enjoyed being around her, but I knew this woman didn't like me. It didn't take a genius to see she felt some type of way about me. The dinner would have been more comfortable if his mother didn't keep glaring at every chance she got. I shouldn't have felt bad because she was doing the same thing to her sister-in-law who seem to not give two rats behind either.

Was this how a Christian supposed to act? Wasn't she, as the first lady, supposed to set the example for a young woman like me? If she had a problem with me, then she should have come out and said it. That's what real women do. It's been obvious she's disliked me way before I showed up with Aden today. As much as she loved her son, the main topic of conversation the entire evening was about Payton and the details on her big extravagant wedding she was having in eleven months. The poor thing was delusional. Her mouth ran a mile a minute about the wedding this and flowers that. It was obvious her fiancé, Rowan, was tired of hearing about the details. Payton had her head too stuck in the clouds to notice. Either he didn't want to get married or it was the fact he recognized me.

You see, I knew Rowan was nervous because he didn't expect to be sitting across the family dinner table from me. I never forgot a face and I'm pretty sure he didn't forget mine either. His eyes nearly fell out his head when he saw me. How could he forget me? He kept telling me how I was the best he'd ever had. Looking at Payton, I could understand why. As casual as he acted when Aden introduced us, there was no introductions needed. I knew Rowan really well. We both played it off like we didn't know each other. At times I found him casting a glance my way. Each time I smirked. I even lifted my foot to rub up and down his leg just for the sake of messing with him. He shifted so many times with uneasiness that Payton asked him if he was okay.

Payton was an attractive woman but too uptight for me. Her hair was perfect, her make-up was spot on and attire pristine. But she appeared to be like one of those Stepford wives. Now I understood why Rowan was stepping out behind her back. There was no way he was getting any nookie from this woman. Not before marriage. And if they had become intimate, it was probably robotic.

For a corporate man, Rowan knew how to please a woman. Most corporate men I'd dealt with were lousy lovers who never measured up to the greatness they said they could deliver to me. But Rowan talked the talked and walked the walk. No wonder Payton was so amped to get this marriage underway. She was trying to lock him down before another woman got her clutches on him. Little did she know he was freely spreading himself amongst the city? I knew if he and I got down so easily, it wasn't his first time stepping out on Payton and I knew it wouldn't be his last.

He wasn't ready for a lifelong commitment. I found this humorous, especially when the Reid family was supposed to be so highly favored. They were considered the leading church family in our community. Still, I wasn't naïve. I knew beyond the greatness they possessed, they weren't perfect. They had skeletons in their closet just like the rest of us. Who knew I would be one for Rowan. He didn't have to worry about me. This would be our little secret, for now.

There did come a moment when Rowan and I were able to talk.

He approached me asking, "Are you stalking me?"

"Stalking?" I said giving him a quizzical gaze.

"That's what I asked."

"Please don't flatter yourself, Rowan. You may have skills in the bedroom but not enough for a sister like me to take time out of my day to stalk you."

"Shhhhhhh," he said looking around to see if anyone heard me. Once he realized we were in the clear he continued. "Then what are you doing here?"

"Aden invited me."

"How long have you been seeing him?" he asked.

Rowan was coming at me like he was my man. I knew I was good and all but maybe he needed to look in the mirror at himself when it came to calling someone a stalker.

"We are just friends."

"With benefits I'm guessing?" he asked in a menacing tone.

"For now?"

"What does that supposed to mean?" he hissed.

Just then Payton decided to walk up with a bright smile. I swear no one could be as happy as she was putting on. Then again, maybe she was. She was under the impression her life was perfect. Poor thing didn't have a clue at the deception surrounding her.

"I see you two are getting to know one another."

"Yes, I was asking her how she met Aden."

"I told him Aden and I met in church."

"Yes, I've seen you there before. Do you enjoy coming to Greater Faith Baptist Church?"

"I sure do. Your father is an amazing preacher. No one can deliver the word quite like he can."

"That is true," she blushed. "I'm so happy to see my brother bring someone home. You know you are the second woman he's ever brought home to meet our parents," she leaned in and said.

"Payton," Rowan hushed.

"Well its true honey. I'm happy to see my brother with someone as beautiful as Juliana. And she's mature. She's not like some of the young minded women I've seen him with in the past."

"Thank you, Payton for the compliment."

"Trust me. My mother is a hard woman to please. It took me a while to gather the nerve to bring Rowan here to meet my parents. But as you can see, it's paid off," she gleamed squeezing his arm.

"I know you are excited about the wedding?" I prodded knowing this had to be getting under Rowan's skin.

"I am. I can't wait for the big day. I'm going to make sure you get an invite too."

"Thank you," I responded.

Rowan smiled stiffly like he couldn't wait for this interaction to be over. So, I decided to help him out with that.

"It was good talking with you, Payton. I'm going to go find your brother."

"He's probably in the kitchen trying to take all the leftovers home," she laughed.

I left both of them, looking back once to see her talking his ear off. Our eyes met for a moment and I turned to find Aden.

Juliana

Aden was gracious enough to walk me to my door as he carried a to-go plate he made me before we left. Payton was right. He was in the kitchen trying to pack up all the leftover food. I was appreciative he was looking out for me as well.

After unlocking the door to my home, I turned to face him. He looked so good. I surveyed him from head to toe. I could stare at this man all night. He was wearing the heck out of those black slacks and button down white shirt. He'd left his jacket in his car after getting comfortable at dinner with his parents.

"Do you like what you see?" he asked, smirking at me, revealing that deep dimple in his left cheek I loved so much.

"I do. You are a very captivating man, Mr. Reid."

Aden was tall with a medium build with his skin a chestnut complexion. His lips were plump, eyes expressive, much like his temperament and his face was clean shaven. When he smiled at me, his teeth blinded me they were so white.

Aden responded with, "I think you are a captivating woman as well Ms. Simmons"

"You think so?"

With his eyes roaming my body, he said, "Oh, yes. You are fine."

This caused me to laugh.

"I appreciate you taking me to your parent's home, even though I know your mother doesn't like me."

"What gave you that impression?" he asked.

"Seriously? If looks could kill, I would be dead already."

"I'm sorry if my mother made you uncomfortable. She doesn't like any women I date."

"So, we are dating? I didn't know this," I quipped.

"I considered this a date. Isn't this what you wanted, to be by my side?" he questioned.

"And you came to this conclusion how?"

"Please, Juliana. I've seen the way you've been throwing yourself at me."

"Throwing myself?" I said laughing at his cockiness.

"Yes. You couldn't wait until I asked you out. I wanted to make your day and give you what you wanted, which was me," he said, arrogantly placing his hand on his chest.

"Conceited, aren't you?"

"No. I'm just observant."

"What else have you observed?" I asked flirtatiously.

"I know you find me irresistible."

"Really?"

"You want to use my body as your very own playground."

"Is that right?" I asked going along with this game of his.

"Let's stop playing around and do this, Juliana."

"By do this, you mean what exactly?"

He chuckled as he looked around, but he didn't say anything.

"Don't be quiet now. You have been talking like you know me, Aden Reid."

"Not my first and last name."

"If I knew your middle name, I would have included that as well."

He smiled bashfully.

"Don't shut down now. Or is it that you know it's not gentlemen like to tell a woman let's do this," I said trying to duplicate his voice.

He chuckled saying, "You got me. I was rude."

"It was beyond rude."

"Please, accept my apology," he said humbly.

"Apology accepted," I smiled.

"You were magnificent company tonight, Juliana. I hope we can do this again soon."

"Thanks for a wonderful evening as well, Mr. Reid."

The both of us stood there in silence, smirking at one another.

"I guess I will be going," he said hesitantly. He turned slowly but I stopped him.

"Wait."

He turned back to face me.

"If I agree to do this, isn't your mother going to disapprove? I mean, you are an innocent preacher's son," I kidded.

"Wow. You're just going to bring my mother into this right now? Talk about a mood killer."

"I'm being real with you. We know your mother is head of your house even though your father is the man of the house. As much as I've tried to get along with her, she can't stand me. I know for sure she doesn't want you to do this with me."

"Look, you don't have to worry about her when you are with me. I'm grown, and I make my own decision. Let's forget about her and talk about you letting me come into your place tonight," he said pointing at my door.

"Do I look like that kind of woman?" I quipped.

I did have a reputation. I was a woman who enjoyed male attention that led to a bedroom a time or two or three or…I mean who's counting. Please understand when I decided to give myself to a man, I did it because I loved the guy. He just so happened to dump me after he took my virginity away from me. He got what he wanted and moved on to the next chick. I can remember like it was yesterday. I was only fifteen years old calling myself in love with this guy. He used me and had the audacity to put what we did in the street. Females were looking at me like I was some kind of slut and guys were looking at me as an easy lay. But I wasn't. I thought I was giving myself to someone I cared for deeply. It took me a long time to get over his betrayal. That incident taught me a lot. It taught me to use a man before they had a chance to use me. And if we ended up using each other, then that's what it was, and I was good with that.

Unfortunately, I have been labeled a whore and not a player like these men out here. I was the female women wanted to keep away from their man, hear them tell it. They were so quick to judge but slow to get to know the real Juliana and the story behind why I was like I was. I guarantee if they took the opportunity to talk to me, most would be able to relate. But none wanted to take that chance on getting close to me for fear I would take their man. This saddened me at times.

I elected to leave love out of the equation forever. That was until here recently. Aden was a distraction for who I really wanted. It had been a long time since I had major feelings for a man, one that I loved but unfortunately couldn't have. Love got you hurt and I didn't like being on the receiving end of that pain.

"Come on, Juliana, let me come in. I know it's late, but I would like to spend some more time with you," Aden said.

I turned to open my door. Gripping a handful of his shirt, I pulled him into my place. I didn't wait for the door to close before I kissed him passionately. His lips were soft. I enjoyed the minty taste of his tongue wrestling with mine. He kicked the door closed and took me into his strong masculine arms.

Between kisses I asked, "Is this what you want?"

"Yes," he said with bated breath.

"How bad?"

"More than you know," he retorted.

"Then let's do this."

Amelia

After putting on my night gown, which I hated
wearing, I climbed into bed. Since Delilah was in my
home I couldn't be as free as I would like. Even in my
own bedroom. She had a habit of popping in my room
like she owned the place. I swear that woman didn't
have any manners. She didn't know what it was to knock
on a closed door. She would waltz her behind in here and
get mad if you said something to her about it. One time,
while me and Carson was making love, she came barging
up in here. Of course, our first reaction was to stop what
we were doing. Hers should have been to bolt out of our
room in embarrassment but instead she chose to stand
there grinning at us.

"Get it you two," was what she said, like we were
going to continue while she watched. She didn't
apologize or say excuse me. She stood there like she was
waiting for somebody to bring her some popcorn, so she
could finish watching what we were doing. Needless to
say, neither of us were able to complete the act that night.
Carson wanted to continue once she left but I was done.
Not only did that completely change my mood but it
ticked me off. We've even locked the door, but she

would knock until Carson opened it. Whatever she had to say was always more important than Carson and I spending time together.

Tonight, was no different. As I climbed in my king size bed, Delilah stood in my room, yet again, trying to talk Carson into buying her a new car.

"What's wrong with the car you have, Dee Dee?" he asked.

"It's running funny. Plus, I saw one I wanted today. It was a black 2016 BMW. You should see it. It's a really nice ride and had my name written all over it."

Then you need to use your name and not ours to get the car, I thought.

"Why are you looking at cars when you supposed to be looking for a place to stay?" Carson asked.

I wanted to pat my baby on the back for that one. Now if she was going to live in the car, then I would go buy it now to get her out of my house.

"I was looking but I happen to see this car when I was searching for a place to stay."

"Did you find a place to stay?" Carson asked.

"I saw a few apartments, but it wasn't up to par. I need to find something nice like this."

"You budget doesn't add up to have a place like this, sis."

"That's why I'm asking you for help. I know I can't afford a house like this, but I can at least have an apartment as close to this as possible."

Was she serious? Yes, she was serious. Dee Dee never lived like this. We didn't live like this either until we worked to get the means to live like this. Did she not grasp the concept? Work for what you want, not have your family pay for it while you relax and do nothing.

"I'm not getting you a new car, Dee Dee."

"Carson?" she whined like she was his teenage child. I rolled my eyes at her.

"But what I will do is give you some money to put down on a nice place. I said nice, not extravagant. And it needs to be one you can pay for by yourself, without my help."

"Why are you doing me like this?" she droned.

"This is what I'm offering. I've told you this, but you keep trying to do more than you need to. Now can you please leave our room, so my wife and I can get some sleep? We had a long day and I would like to spend some alone time with her without any more interruptions."

Delilah gawked at me and then back at her brother before exiting our room. She didn't say another word, which was fine with me. Carson got out of bed and closed the door behind her.

"Lock it," I told him.

"But..."

"But nothing. I don't want her barging up in here again. She doesn't know how to knock."

Carson did as I asked and locked the door.

"She's getting on my last nerve. I'm sick of her. I don't know why I agreed to let her stay here."

"You did it because you love me," Carson said, climbing back in the bed next to me.

"I do love you, honey but your sister has to go. She's been here for six months. How long does it take for someone to find a place?"

"She's having a hard time."

"No, I'm having a hard time with having another woman in my house acting like it's hers. We've worked to have this life and that's what she needs to do instead of playing the role of a moocher. If you ask me, I think she's stalling."

"Stalling for what?" Carson asked.

"Six months is a great indicator don't you think, especially when you are giving her the money to put down on a place. And two, she can find a new car to drive but she can't find somewhere to live. What it is, she wants to live here with us permanently."

"I don't know."

"I do and that's a no. I'm not having it."

"Amelia, honey, you know her husband just died."

"That was ten months ago, Carson."

"They were together for quite some time. Losing her husband and then her place to live was a lot for her."

"She let the house go into foreclosure. She had the money to pay that house off from his insurance policy, but she chose to spend all that money on her car and clothes, shoes, jewelry, you name it."

She's been depressed," Carson said making excuses for her.

"Well, I'm getting depressed having her here. All I see is a grown woman who wants her brother to take care of her like her husband did and that's not your place, honey. I don't understand why you feel like you have to do this for her anyway. You've went above and beyond what you had to do for her. She's taking advantage of your kindness."

"I'm the only family she has left."

"It seems like you have become her new man and not her family," I countered.

"Amelia, that sounds crazy."

"I'm not saying it like that. I mean you are supporting her. Her deceased husband supported her and the man before him supported her. When is she going to learn to support herself? This is 2017 for goodness sake. Women know how to do things for themselves."

"Not everybody is like you."

Smiling, I said, "Thank you, honey."

"It's true."

"I know but I bet you she will learn how to be independent if you cut her off," I retorted. "You are an enabler."

Carson sighed in frustration.

"I'm sorry to come at you like this, honey, but I've had it. Dee Dee has to go."

"I don't know if I can kick my own sister out. It's not like we don't have the room here," my husband pleaded.

"Carson, give her a deadline. Tell her she has two weeks to move out or you will have to evict her. If you don't do it, I will."

I could see Carson's didn't like it, but I didn't care. I wanted my house back. I wanted it to be just me and him. Both of our children were out of the home and these were the days I was looking forward to spending with him. With Delilah here, it was like raising another child. She was causing a wedge between us and before I allowed her to ruin my marriage, I would get rid of her, which in turn would eliminate the problem.

"I'll talk to her," Carson finally said.

I leaned over and kissed him on the cheek.

"Thank you, honey. You have made me a very happy wife," I said smiling at him.

He smiled but still seemed to be a bit upset by this conversation. I didn't know the hold Delilah had over him. This was more than a brother and a sister connecting. This was something else. His worried expression told me that, but I decided to leave well enough alone for the night. I'd got what I wanted out of this conversation and that was Carson agreeing to ask his sister to leave.

Skye

I decided to show up early to the restaurant and arrived around 6:30 in the morning. Seth wondered where I was going since I usually left my home around 7:20 but I told him I wanted to go to the gym first. Making the lie look real, I got dressed in my workout gear and brought my duffle bag to change into my clothes at the office. He didn't bother to second guess me and took me at my word. I didn't know if it was because he didn't care or because he had other things on his mind that didn't concern me.

I was extremely nervous about meeting with this woman. I didn't know what to expect. Was she tall or short? Was she a thick sister or skinnier than me? How was her hair? Was she prettier than me? All these questions were rumbling through my mind as I tried to avoid the ultimate question. Was this woman really sleeping with my husband?

"Coffee," the waitress asked startling me. "I'm sorry. I didn't mean to scare you."

With my hand on my chest, I said, "It's okay. That's what I get for daydreaming too much."

"Would you like some coffee?" she asked again.

"Please," I gestured to the empty white mug in front of me. I watched as she poured the hot liquid into the cup.

"Are you ready to order?"

"Not yet. I'm still waiting on someone," I told her looking at my watch to see it was close to seven.

As soon as the waitress walked away, I heard the ding of the door indicating a patron was entering. I saw a thick sister walk in looking around. For a second, we made eye contact and she started in my direction. This couldn't be the woman Seth was sleeping with, could it? She was twice as big as me. I was a size nine and she looked to be a size eighteen. I knew the media was all about weight and the skinnier you were, the more appealing they considered you but in this case the media was wrong. I tried to never judge but probably have been guilty a time or two. But this woman, I had to admit, for a thick sister, she was very attractive. With butter brown skin, curves for days, and long hair pulled up in a cute top knot, this woman was absolutely gorgeous. Her attire didn't make me feel any better. Here I was dressed in my workout gear and she came strolling up in here making me look like a charity case. With a pair of black ripped jeans on, a white graphic tee which said girl power covered by a black leather jacket and a pair of fresh white

Yeezies on her feet, she was styling. Her make-up and her hair was done to perfection as silver hoops dangled from her earlobes. Even though it wasn't many patrons here in the restaurant, the few that were here took notice of this vivacious woman.

When she approached my table she asked, "Are you Skye?"

"Yes, I am," I answered.

"I'm Fatima, the woman you've been speaking with," she said confidently.

She held her hand out to me to shake mine. I didn't know if she was being nice or condescending. This wasn't two women getting together to catch up on old times. This was meeting the woman claiming to be sleeping with my husband. Looking upward at her, I hesitantly took her hand into mine.

"Please, have a seat," I gestured towards the chair across from me.

She pulled the seat out and sat before me putting her *Gucci* handbag in the chair to her right. My eyes swallowed in her splendor. Now that we were adjacent to one another, I could see she was more attractive than ever and this made my own insecurities creep in.

"I wish I could say it was nice to meet you, but you do understand, due to the circumstances, I can't say that," I said trying to portray confidence when in actuality I was a bit intimidated.

66

"I understand. I'm glad you are choosing to handle this like a grown woman," she responded.

Was that a dig, I thought? Did she do things like sleep with married men often for women to not act like a grown woman to her?

"I'm not sure if I could be as demure as you have been," she added.

"Trust me, it's very difficult sitting here with you this morning."

The waitress approached again and asked Fatima what she would like to drink.

"Coffee, please. And I'm going to need a lot of cream and sugar."

The waitress went to retrieve her morning wake up drink and our eyes connected again with neither of us not knowing what to say to one another.

"Do you want me to start and shall I," she asked.

"Please, I don't mind if you start. I would love to hear what you have to say for yourself."

She twisted her lips and sniggered a bit. She didn't seem none too happy by my response. At this point I didn't care. She needed to understand I was the wife here, not the other woman sleeping with someone's husband.

The waitress walked up with the coffee pot and poured it into the white coffee mug in front of her. The waitress placed more cups of creamer and packs of sugar for my unwanted guest.

"Are you ladies ready to order?" the woman asked us.

"Yes, I'll order your south western omelet," Fatima ordered.

"Do you just want the omelet or would you like the special which comes with a side of pancakes?"

"The special sounds great. And can I get extra salsa for my omelet?"

"You sure can," the kind woman said. "And you ma'am?"

"I'll take two eggs over easy, some toast, and two strips of bacon. That will do it for me," I said. "And can you make mine to go, please."

"Sure. I can do that for you. I'll be back soon with your orders," the woman smiled as she exited our table.

I wasn't hungry at all but ordered anyway. I got my food to go because I knew there was no way I was going to be able to consume anything as nervous as my stomach was. Getting this coffee down was a task in itself. My appetite was gone but I knew maybe later this morning I would want something.

"If I would've known Seth was married, I would have never got involved with him," Fatima admitted.

"But you know now." I said flippantly.

"That's true and I know what I'm saying doesn't mean anything because you are the one who got hurt here."

Passively I asked, "Where did you meet my husband?"

"We met at my job. I'm a bartender at a local bar here."

"Really?"

"Yes, I've been there for four years now."

"Who made the first move?"

"He did," she answered.

"An attractive woman like you, I know men hit on you all the time. What was it about my husband that made you take things further with a patron?"

She shifted but it wasn't done like she was uncomfortable. She did this like she was trying to keep her cool. It was obvious she didn't like the way I was coming at her and again I didn't care.

"For one, he's a very attractive man as you very well know."

"You don't have attractive men come to the bar where you work?"

"Yes, but it was something about Seth that appealed to me."

"You didn't see that ring on his finger?" I questioned.

"He wasn't wearing one."

I drew in a deep breath with that revelation. Not wearing his ring was a sure sign he was trying to get with another woman. Why else would a married man take off his ring?

She continued with, "It was obvious by his multiple advances towards me he was interested in me."

"Multiple?"

"Yes. I denied his advances for a while but eventually his persistence wore me down. The next thing I knew we were going to dinner together," she explained brazenly as she leaned back in her seat and crossed her legs.

"Did you sleep with him the first time you guys got together?"

"Yes."

Her answered shocked me. I asked because I was curious, but I didn't expect her to say yes. What kind of woman was she to sleep with a man the first time she went out with him? Who am I kidding? She's the kind of woman who sleeps with someone else's husband. So, why would I expect her to respect herself enough to keep her legs closed on the first date?

Clearing my throat, I asked, "You didn't think you were lowering yourself, you know, sleeping with a strange man the first night?"

Smiling coyly, she said, "I didn't think I was lowering myself. You see, I do what I want, when I want, and with whom I want. I'm a grown woman who takes care of herself and if anyone has a problem with that, they can kiss my…"

"Here's your food, ladies," the waitress interrupted. Fatima smirked as she glared at me.

Placing Fatima's plates of steaming food before her and my container filled with my meal, the waitress asked, "Is there anything else I can get you?"

"No, I think we are good," Fatima answered.

When the waitress left us along again, I looked back across the table at Fatima who leaned forward to place the napkin in her lap.

"You were saying," I said giving her permission to speak.

"Skye, it's obvious you don't like me or respect me for that matter."

"You would be corrected," I agreed.

"I know it's because I'm with your husband."

"You are sleeping with my husband. You are not with him. Let's get that clear," I corrected.

"Like I was saying, you are angry because we are together," she said, ignoring the fact I proclaimed Seth as mine, which he was per the marriage vows we spoke to each other and the marriage certificate certifying such.

"Your problem is with him, not me, Skye," she told me.

"Both of you are my problem. Seth for having the audacity to step outside of our marriage. And you for continuing your unscrupulous affair with him even after you found out he was committed to me."

"Committed?" she giggled.

"As far as I'm concerned, you could have been a one night stand that he discarded like yesterday's trash."

Fatima sucked her teeth as her eyes became slits.

"I guess I'm recycled trash since he keeps using me over and over again."

I gave her a bitter gaze.

"Used, isn't that what you said? He's using you. He made me his wife."

Leaning in closer, she asked, "For how long?"

I frowned.

"It's a matter of time before this used item becomes a permanent fixture. Who do you think he's thinking about when he's lying next to you at night? Heck, sometimes your husband can't make it through a night without sneaking out of your bed to talk to me. He just wants to hear my voice he tells me."

Her words stung. I'd thought the same thing last night when Seth came to bed, wondering if he was thinking of her. He took his shower, crawled in the bed and turned his back to me without so much as a good night kiss. All the red flags were there indicating he was drifting away from me. I knew our marriage was in jeopardy, but I'd been denying it hoping things would get better. Hearing Fatima say he was thinking about her almost made me want to burst into tears. But I couldn't give her the satisfaction of knowing how devastated I was over this. My eyes betrayed me anyway. A lone tear dripped from my right eye and I quickly swiped it away. Fatima's harden demeanor softened when she saw this.

"Look, Skye. I know how you are feeling."

"Do you?" I snapped thinking she didn't have a clue how I was feeling.

"Yes, I do. My husband cheated on me with my best friend. He married her, and they recently had a child together."

I looked at her in disbelief.

Leaning back in her chair again, she lowered her head and said, "Not only did I lose my husband, I lost my best friend of eleven years."

Her mood mirrored mine in that moment. For the first time since she was here she showed some empathy. For a moment our pain matched. We connected. She'd been where I was now. Then why do this to me? Granted in the beginning she didn't know he was married but now she did. Why continue with the affair? Why sit here and give me the impression my husband was leaving me for her?

With sadden eyes, she said, "I didn't mean for any of this to happen. I truly didn't. You can believe me or not. That's up to you. I was out of line for the things I said to you. I know I was reacting to how you were treating me, which was warranted. Yet, I stilled inflicted pain on you and I'm sorry for that."

The waitress walked up to our table again.

"You ladies enjoying your food?"

Not answering I asked, "Do you think you can bring our bill please?"

"And I'm going to need a to-go container as well," Fatima added, having not touched a morsel of her breakfast.

The waitress brought us our tickets and we paid, not saying anything else to one another. Once our transactions were done and food all wrapped up to go, Fatima spoke.

"What I'm about to say may sound crazy but I'm going to say it anyway. You know Seth is not done with me, right?"

I titled my head in discomfort but said nothing.

"If I'm correcting in my thinking, I feel like you want proof if his infidelity. The word of a strange woman is not enough to go on, is that correct?" she asked.

Hesitantly, I nodded.

"I can call you when he's at my home the next time," Fatima suggested. "This way you can see for yourself and maybe that can help you get a better understanding of what you need to do."

Seeing him with her was only going to further devastate me but what other choice did I have. I couldn't keep pretending like he wasn't cheating on me. The facts were adding up, but I was still trying to make our marriage equal a happily ever after.

"Are you really in love with Seth?" I asked.

Unblinking she said, "No."

I nodded.

"Seth has been fun, but I don't want him for myself. If he's willing to cheat on you, I know he will do the same to me. Most women don't understand that when they step into the role of wife, after being his side piece. I get it because I lived it. My ex-best friend thinks things are perfect in her marriage to my ex-husband, but I know otherwise. I know because I've heard he's doing her the same way he did me. What is the saying? How you get him is how you lose him?"

Fatima made perfect since.

"I'm doing this for you. I know you don't want to know but you have to find out in order to move on. And I don't want you to think I'm doing this because I want him all to myself. I don't. I'm using him for some needs he's giving me for the moment. As for a permanent relationship, I'm not interested."

"When do you think he's going to come over?"

"He talked like he wanted to come over tonight," she advised.

"Do you still have my number?" I asked.

"I do," she answered.

"Then call me when Seth is there."

Amelia

I had another bad dream. I woke up this morning with something in my spirit that wasn't sitting right with me. I stared at the chandelier hanging over my bed and wondered why I felt uneasy. I didn't know if this feeling had to do with the conversation Carson and I had last night or the fact my son was fooling around with a Jezebel.

I climbed out of bed and dropped to my knees. Closing my eyes, I started praying to the good Lord. This was my favorite time to speak to Him, praise Him, and thank Him for all He'd done for me.

"Good morning Father. First, thank you for waking me up to see another day. I'm coming to you this morning with heaviness on my heart. My spirit is shaken and I'm not sure why Lord. I know you will reveal it to me. I ask that you keep my family under your wings of Grace, Father God. Protect them in a mighty way, Lord. Continue to guide us even when we sometimes get off the road for which we supposed to go. Lead us Father. Direct our path and give us the strength to endure any obstacles that come our way. I thank you for what you have done and what you are doing in our lives, Father

God. I ask you these things in the precious name of Jesus. Amen."

"Amen," Carson said.

When I opened my eyes, I saw him looking down at me as he stood by the bed.

"I love it when you pray," he said.

Rising to my feet, I walked over to him and gave him a peak on the lips as I said, "Thank you, honey and good morning."

"Good morning to you, honey."

"I didn't hear you come in."

"When you are having a talk with the Lord, all things around you cease. That's a great thing. I stood here and closed my eyes with you."

I smiled at him, but I guess my smile wasn't my usual jubilant smile because Carson asked me what was wrong.

"I have this uneasy feeling and you know when I get like this, I become afraid because it usually means something bad is going to happen."

"Does this have anything to do with what we discussed last night?"

"I don't know," I said.

"Honey, everything is going to be fine. I'm doing better. The church is doing very well. You are looking wonderful as ever. Our kids are great. And I've decided to give my sister a deadline."

I gave him a skeptical expression. First, I had to see him give his sister an ultimatum before I believed him. And as for our children, I knew they were well, but my son needed to get it together. I still couldn't get over the fact he brought that woman up in my house.

"Amelia," Carson called.

"Yes."

"What did that look for?"

"It's nothing."

"It's written all over your face," he said rubbing lotion on his hands.

Chuckling, I said, "I keep forgetting you've known me long enough to read me."

"Twenty-five years. So, let whatever you have going on in that mind of yours go. Get dressed for the day and walk in the spirit of His goodness."

"Okay, Carson," I said reaching for the covers to make my side of the bed.

"Do you have any plans today?" he asked.

"I'm supposed to have lunch with Elaine today."

Elaine was my best friend and was also married to my brother Diego. We'd been friends since high school. Everybody thought we were sisters because we favored each other so much. Plus, we lied and told everyone we were. Elaine and I had the same cocoa complexion, thick hips, and small waistline. When she married my brother, people thought we were committing incest. It was harder getting out of the lie than telling it, which was the way of the world. Lies always came back to haunt you. Now, most understood Diego was actually my brother and Elaine and I were great friends. I was happy she'd become my sister-in-law. Through all the trials and tribulations, the one constant that has been there is my friendship with her.

"You make sure to tell Elaine I said hello. I haven't seen her in a while. I'm used to seeing her all the time."

"She's been busy building her home interior business. She's been pressuring me to get our home re-done. If she wasn't my best friend, I would take offense to that."

Putting on his necktie Carson asked, "Why don't you let her do it?"

"Because I think my home is fine the way it is. Where do you think she got her style from? She used to come to me asking questions on decorating and even her clothing," I said going over to the dresser and pulling out some undergarments to put on after my shower.

Carson chuckled and asked, "You afraid she's going to out do you?"

"Don't make me hurt you this morning, honey. Just because you are a Pastor and I'm the First Lady don't mean we won't scrap up in this room?"

"Look at my baby resorting back to her old ways."

"You know I still can. Besides, another reason why I don't feel like we need this is because I don't want anyone else talking about how much money it looks like we are spending. People are already running their mouths about this house and the cars we have. There's no need to give them something else to talk about."

I don't know what it was about church folk talking about someone else's blessing. Yes, Carson and I use to live in a house no bigger than a thousand square feet. But last year, we decided to upgrade and get the home of our dreams. People automatically thought we used the churches money to purchase this home. People forgot before Carson worked at the church full time, he worked as a manager on a construction site and I use to run a daycare center before an electrical fire caused it to burn down. We knew way back, before we became Pastor and First Lady, one day we wanted our dream home. We saved for years putting away money to go towards this home. It also helped I'd received an insurance settlement from the fire of my daycare center. Then two years ago when my parents passed away, I inherited a substantial amount of assets along with my dad's company whom I shared with my brother. I was more of a silent partner while he ran the company today, which was very successful. I couldn't help the timing of Carson becoming Pastor of our church and the two of us purchasing our home which happened around the same time.

I didn't know why I let what people said bother me. I used to not care but since I've stepped into this role of First Lady, I've always wanted to be respected. I never wanted anyone to question what was going on in my home or our finances. Really, it was none of their business.

Carson commented on the subject saying, "Tell those people God has blessed us."

"Like they are going to believe that. People are quick to believe the negative more than the positive. Some want to believe we are stealing from the church and using the money to live this life of luxury and I don't like it. I tell you it's getting harder and harder to keep a smile on my face each time I step foot up in that sanctuary."

I could feel my anger bubbling to the surface. Carson noticed and continued.

"Honey, don't get upset."

"I can't help it. I feel like my world is getting ready to fall apart."

"You like to control things and right now the things that are happening are out of your control. You have to stop letting so many things get to you. You've been upset about my sister being here, about the church folks talking and about Aden being with Juliana."

"That Jezebel is using our son, Carson," I said sitting on the side of the bed.

"You don't know that."

"You know this woman's reputation. Do you really want us to be linked with someone like her?" I questioned.

"What do you mean someone like her?"

"Do you really need me to sp3ll it out?"

"Amelia, you really need to watch what you are saying. Not even five minutes ago you were talking about the church folk talking about us and here you are doing the same thing."

"This is different."

"No, it's not," he retorted.

"This is my child."

"And the church members may think it's their hard earn money we are spending. Talk is talk, especially when you are talking about somebody."

"She's promiscuous."

"Don't forget where we came from. It's not like our sexual partners from the past are on a short list."

"So, you are saying I was a whore?"

"That's not what I'm saying," he defended.

"That's exactly what it sounds like to me. You don't have to remind me of the partners I've had in my past. Granted, I can't count them on my fingers and toes, but I bet you any amount of money Juliana can't count her conquests on hers, mine, yours, and Aden's fingers and toes put together."

"Her having more partners than you, makes her worse than you?" he questioned.

"Yes," I answered.

"A sin is a sin. You are sounding like a hypocrite."

"Whatever, Carson. I'm not happy she's with Aden. All she wants to do is take our son on her next great adventure."

"Next great adventure," Carson said chuckling. "What is she, an amusement park?"

"Yes, with all those twist and curves she has, her body is an amusement park. Do you know how many people enter her each year?"

"Amelia, stop it."

"I'm just saying. Aden is my only son. I don't want him caught up in no mess. He needs to settle down with a nice church girl."

"You do know the more you push him in one direction, the more he's going to go in the opposite," Carson responded.

"Then you talk with him. You are his father. Tell him what he needs to do."

"That boy is a grown man. All we can do is guide him. We can't make him do anything he doesn't want to do. You are going to have to cut the apron strings and let him live his life."

I knew Carson was right, but I wasn't going to admit it.

"Honey, you have to let this go or you're going to drive yourself crazy."

"That's easier said than done."

"I know but you can do it. I want my wife around for another twenty five years. I don't need stress taking you away from me," he said approaching me and wrapping his arms around me.

As comforted as I felt in his arms, I still had this uneasy feeling and hoped whatever the Lord was trying to warn me about, it wouldn't be tragic to our family.

Skye

I was a little distracted today to say the least in regard to my personal life and the downfall of my marriage. I can't deny the breakfast this morning with Fatima did play a major role in my mood today. To boost it up a bit, I decided to ask my husband out to lunch since today was my half day. I thought it would be nice if we spent some time together. How surprised was I to he had the day off? Seth didn't mention anything to me about taking a day off and neither did Fatima.

I felt like an utter fool. Here I was, his wife, calling to speak with him and didn't even know he wasn't there. I should have been the first person he told. I could feel the embarrassment of the situation through the phone with his secretary and I wanted to hang up without even saying good bye. I played it off like I forgot about it. But how could I forget something I didn't even know about.

I knew Seth was with her. I wondered was this his first time doing this or had he done this often. I wouldn't know because I was wrapped up in my own work day to have time to worry about what he was doing during the day.

I tossed the pen I was holding to my desk in frustration and lowered my head on my hands as I leaned forward on my desk. I wanted to cry so bad but knew this was not the time or place for a breakdown.

Nurse Camille gently tapped on my open door as she peeked her head in snapping me out of my thoughts. I looked up and she said, "Dr. Holden, your patient is in room 102 if you are ready."

"Okay, Camille. I'll be right there,"

When my nurse got ready to walk away, I stopped her by calling out to her.

"Yes," she answered.

"Have you seen the lotion I had on my desk?"

She walked in and looked at the spot I usually kept it because the both of us used it due to us washing our hands so much. The hard water in the building was terrible on our skin.

"It was there Friday," she responded.

"I know. I don't know what happened to it."

"Just so you know, I didn't take it," Camille said putting her hand to her chest.

"Oh, I wasn't accusing you at all. I trust you. Besides we take turns buying this lotion when we run out. I don't mind anyone else using it but don't take something that doesn't belong to you," I said.

"I totally agree. I wanted you to know it wasn't me."

I could see the street side of Camille coming out and I had to giggle to myself.

"What?" she asked.

"I just love you," I told her.

"I love you, too," she said smiling. "I didn't want anything like a bottle of lotion to ruin our friendship."

"You must think little of me if you believe I would let something like lotion come between us. You know me better than that."

"I do," Camille agreed.

"We've worked together for a few years now. You are my right hand person and have become a great friend to me. I appreciate you."

"Thank you for telling me that," she smiled. "Would you like to go have a drink after we leave here?"

"I need one today," I mumbled.

"We can go now if you want. I'm always down to get my drink on."

"Let me think about it. I'll let you know in a bit. Is that okay?"

"Sure. I don't have anything to do once I leave here," she said walking to the doorway. She turned and said, "Skye, are you okay?"

"Yes, I'm good," I lied.

She looked at me skeptically and said, "Just in case you aren't, I'm here if you need to talk."

"Thank you, Camille."

Getting myself together, I gathered my laptop and entered room 102.

"Hello, Mr. Evans. My name is…"

"Skye?" the male voice said interrupting me.

"Yes," I said frowning, not quite sure how this gentleman knew my name. What I was concentrating on was the infant he was holding in his arms.

"It's me, Dante,"

I didn't respond studying his face but still couldn't place him.

"You remember, Dante from high school. I used to wear the sweaters all the time with collar shirts and black rimmed glasses," he said chuckling.

As if a light bulb went off, my mouth fell open and I said, "Dante," still looking at him questioningly because he didn't look like the same church boy I went to school with.

"That's me in flesh. How are you doing?"

"I'm good," I retorted looking at the most scrumptious man I'd ever seen. He'd come a long way from the nerdy boy in high school. Dante stood tall, looking to be about 6'1" with the smoothest coffee complexion. His shoulders were broad, and body seemed chiseled. I guess I was staring too hard for him to say his next statement.

"I look different right?" he asked bouncing the baby in his arms.

"You sure do. Getting old has definitely suited you."

"So, you are impressed with what you see?" he asked in a way that made me shift uncomfortably.

"You look great," I stuttered.

I knew this man wasn't flirting with me when it was obvious he was in some type of relationship for him to be bringing a baby to this appointment.

"You look amazing as always," he complimented causing me to blush.

"Thank you," I said nervously walking over to the counter and placing the laptop down before I dropped it. I had to pay attention to something else other than how fine this man was.

"I see you are a doctor now. Congratulations. That's a big accomplishment."

"Yes, I've always wanted to treat children even though I don't have any of my own," I said wondering why in the world did I offered this piece of information about myself.

He responded by saying, "I don't have any kids either."

I looked at the baby he was holding, and Dante looked at him too.

"Oh, this is my little nephew. My sister had to go to court today regarding child support. She couldn't be in two places at one time. My schedule was flexible, so I offered to bring him today."

"That's sweet."

"Anytime I can get to spend with this little guy is great," he said looking at the infant who was drooling all over himself. "Isn't that right Sebastian?" The baby smile widened.

Seeing how Dante was interacting with his nephew was so adorable and refreshing because I didn't see many men in this office. Most times I dealt with the children's mother or grandmother's but hardly ever fathers and never uncles.

"Why am I seeing this cutie pie today?" I asked.

"He's been coughing a lot and seems to be congested. Last night he started running a temperature," Dante told me.

"Can you lay him down on the examining table for me please?"

Dante gently placed his nephew on his back. I could tell already this baby was going to be a breeze to examine. He wasn't crying at all and seemed to be a very playful and happy baby. He laid before me like a champ with his big brown eyes looking up at me.

Putting the stethoscope to his chest, Sebastian playfully gripped my hand and looked up at me with a big grin on his little face. I happily smiled back at him.

Listening at his chest, I asked, "Do you know how high his temperature was?"

"I think she said 102.3," Dante answered.

Placing the ThermoScan in the babies' ear, I quickly took his temperature as I asked, "Has your sister been giving him anything for his fever?"

"She's been giving him Tylenol. She gave him some right before we came here."

I nodded and continued to examine the baby. It was cute because when I leaned down to look in his ears, he grabbed a handful of my hair trying to put it in his mouth.

"No, Sebastian," Dante said, and his nephew ignored him as another smile spread across his face.

"It's okay. I should have pulled my hair back."

"All he's doing is flirting with you. He must find you as attractive as I do."

Our eyes connected for a feeling moment but then I continued to examine his nephew. I was going to pretend I didn't hear what he said.

"I'm all done," I said picking up Sebastian. Passing his nephew to him, Dante took the baby into his arms.

"He has a slight ear infection which could have occurred due to his cold. His lungs are clear, and he doesn't have a temperature now. I'm going to send a prescription for to the pharmacy for the ear infection which should help with his cold as well. She can continue giving him the Tylenol if his fever comes back. Of course, keep plenty of fluids in him but it seems your sister is doing all the right things," I explained.

"Did you hear that little man? You are going to be fine."

The baby smiled at his uncle all the while trying to grab his face.

"I'll schedule an appointment for her to bring him back in ten days, so we can make sure everything is good."

"Thank you so much, Skye."

"You are welcome. You have a beautiful nephew," I said picking up my laptop. "It was good seeing you again."

Walking to exit the room, Dante stopped me.

"Wait."

"Yes."

"I know this may be totally wrong of me, but do you think I can take you out to dinner?"

This surprised me. A part of me was flattered and got excited at his invitation. That was until my husband Seth crept into my mind.

"I'm sorry. I can't. I'm married," I told him.

"Oh, I'm sorry. I didn't know," he said looking down at my ring finger to see the diamond. I felt like he noticed it earlier but was taking a chance in asking me anyway to see what I would say.

"It's okay. I do appreciate the offer."

"What about lunch? Just old friends catching up with one another," he tried to persuade me.

The fact of the matter was we weren't ever friends. We just went to school together.

"I don't know," I stressed.

"Please," he said begging. "And I'm not a man who begs."

I smiled and said, "Okay. I don't see any harm in that."

"Great. I can call you," he told me.

"But you don't have my number."

"I don't, do I," he said looking flustered.

Was I making this man nervous?

I reached in my lab coat and pulled out my business card.

"Here's my number."

"Great. I'll call you soon. I can't wait to catch up with you."

"It was good seeing you, Dante."

With that I left the room, feeling happier than I had in a while. This very attractive man wanted to spend time with me, when my very own husband didn't. I was going to bask in this feeling because I knew once I got home, things were definitely going to take a turn for the worst.

Juliana

I was surprised it took him this long to show up at my place. He must've known I had company and waiting in the cut for his chance to swing by. He didn't want to interrupt which was respectful on his part. No sooner than Aden left, he was knocking feverishly on my door. When I peeked through the peep hole, I had to smirk knowing why he was on my doorstep.

"Good morning," I said happily in my pink sweat pants and a cut off tee showing off my amazing abs.

"What do you thinking you are doing?" he said busting into my place.

"Come in, Carson," I said shutting the door behind him. When I turned to face him, he was glaring at me.

"How could you show up to my house with my son?"

"Was something wrong with that?" I asked innocently.

"Yes, something was wrong with that? What do you think you are doing?"

"I'm living my life," I said walking over to my love seat and sitting down.

"You are doing this on purpose to get back at me."

"Don't flatter yourself, Carson."

"Why else would you choose Aden and not all the other men who are interested in you?"

"Your son asked me to dinner and I accepted. I didn't know until I said yes that the dinner was going to be at your home. It would have been rude to back out. You seem jealous?"

"I'm not jealous of my own son."

"Maybe you should be. I thought you were good at satisfying me but Aden," I said fanning myself with my hand, "that man knows how to…"

Carson charged towards me. Before I knew it, he had his hand around my throat.

"Shut up about my son," he mumbled through clenched teeth.

"If you wanted it ruff, Carson, all you had to do was ask," I struggled to say, as his fingers tightened around my throat.

Once he saw I wasn't shook, he let me go and darted across the room away from me. I said that about Aden to get under Carson's skin, which worked but what I said was far from the truth. After Aden's lackluster performance last night, I didn't want Aden touching me again. As cocky as he was, was as disappointing as he delivered. Last night he got zeroes across the board. Aden was a feeble replica of the real thing and was only my stepping stone to getting closer to Carson.

"I don't know why you are mad. You told me you didn't want to be with me anymore."

"And you know why. I'm married," he replied.

"Were you not married when you slid between my thighs?"

He didn't answer but he didn't have to.

"How long have we been having an affair?"

"I don't know," he avoided.

"It's been eight months. Now, all of a sudden you've started feeling a smidgen of guilt and decided to call things off between us."

"You knew it wasn't going to last," he said.

"Did I? Because I was under the impression you cared about me."

"I do."

"You ended it like I never meant anything to you. You know I love you and you treated me like I was disposable."

"I didn't mean for you to feel l like this. I didn't mean for any of this to happen. If I would have known you were going to catch feelings, I would have never done this."

"You see. You didn't say because of your wife, you wouldn't have done this. You said because of my feelings. This lets me know you still love me."

Carson told me he loved me on several occasions and I believed him. Now he was backtracking like that never happened.

"What, did Jesus come down and have a talk to you about your sins?"

"My conscious kicked in. I made a mistake by being with you," he explained.

"And you've asked God to forgive you for your transgression, right?" I asked condescendingly.

Carson scowled at me.

"I'm going to pay for what I've done to my wife by being with you and I'm ready for the repercussion behind that. But what I won't do is continue to do wrong with you when it's my wife whom I love."

"Then why are you here?" I asked.

"My son. If I didn't know any better, I would think you are trying to get back at me."

"And maybe it could be I just like him."

99

"Leave him alone, Juliana," he said looking at me menacingly.

"And if I don't?" I challenged.

I know the good pastor wasn't standing in my home threatening me.

"You will find out if you continue this farce of a relationship with Aden."

"Carson, you hold no cards here. If anything, I hold them all. You have a lot more to lose than I do. Like your snobby little wife and your naïve congregation. What do you think any of them would think if they found out you've been having an affair with me?"

He glared at me without saying anything. A knock at the door broke our staring match and his eyes widen at the possibility of getting caught. I wanted to open the door so whoever was on the other side could see him here with me but now was not the time for that.

I stood to my feet and told him, "Go to my room. I'll call you when it's clear."

He wasted no time scurrying from the living room to my bedroom as the doorbell sounded again.

Juliana

This was starting out to be a weird day. First, Carson shows up unannounced and now Rowan decided to show his face here today. He didn't wait for me to say come in, good morning, how you doing, nothing. He brushed pass me and rushed into my place like it was his.

"I didn't invite you in," I told him.

"You didn't have to. I'm here and we need to talk."

"Talk about what, Rowan."

"Us."

"Us. There is no us. You and I knew that going in remember?"

"I know this but you being with Aden is too close to comfort and I'm going to need to you to call it quits with him."

"I need to be calling it quits with you. Do you think we are going to keep doing this?"

He pressed his lips tightly together as he began thinking about what I said.

"You are marrying a preacher's kid. Right now, it's just cheating but in a few months, it's going to be adultery. Is that what you want?"

"You know what I want?"

"Remind me because I don't."

Rowan approached me and pulled me into his arms.

"I want you, Juliana. Seeing you last night excited me but it also ticked me off when I realized you were there with Aden."

"I'm not going to play side piece to you for the rest of my life. I deserve happiness too."

"I know."

"Then you should also know this has to end. I like Aden."

"But you love me," he reminded me.

I didn't respond. Mainly because I didn't want Carson to hear the answer to that. I didn't mind all this other talk we were doing but whether I loved Rowan was not information I wanted him to know.

"You have to leave," I said soft.

Rowan planted his lips onto mine. We kissed deep and passionately and for a moment I forgot all about Carson being in my bedroom. Breaking from the embrace I back out of his arms. He licked his lips like he was trying to savor the lasting effects I had on him.

"Let me make love to you."

"I have someone coming over. You don't want to be caught here."

"Is it Aden?" he asked angrily.

"No," I answered.

"Then call your company and tell him your plans are canceled so we can hang out for a while," he said approaching me again.

I back away saying, "I'm sorry but I can't do that. They are probably on their way already."

"Can I come over later?"

"Call me and I'll let you know."

He glared at me for a moment. Then he nodded.

"Okay. I'll call you. You better answer or I'm coming over here."

"I'll answer, I promise."

He kissed me again and as he begin to make his way to the door, we both heard something coming from my bedroom. That caused Rowan to pause.

"What was that?"

"I don't know."

He frowned and turned to face me fully as he looked in the direction of my bedroom.

"Do you got someone here?" he asked angrily.

"No," I stammered

"Then why are you so nervous all of a sudden."

"Rowan?"

"Is that why you are trying to get me out of here so fast because you already have a man here with you."

"No, please. Don't do this."

Rowan head in the direction of my bedroom. I jumped in front of him to try to stop him, pushing him in his chest as he moved me back like I was made of nothing.

"Stop, Rowan. Don't do this."

"Who is it, Juliana? Who do you have here?"

As we got closer to the doorway to my room, Carson walked out.

Juliana

All I could do was stand there and allow my eyes to bounce between the two men glaring at one another. The silence was deafening and felt like the temperature in the room dropped a few degrees from the frigid demeanor present at the moment.

"You?" Rowan questioned. "Pastor Reid, what are you doing here?"

Rowan not only looked surprised, but he also look shook. His eyes were wide with fear as the father of the woman who he was marrying was catching him here with me.

"I can ask you the same thing, son."

"I...I can explain," Rowan stammered.

"How could you do Payton like this?" She loves you with every fiber of her being."

"I know and I'm sorry. I didn't mean for any of this to happen," Rowan explained.

"It didn't sound like that to me. It sounded like you were over here to sleep with this woman again."

"I.. I.." Rowan continued to stutter as he stuffed his hands deep down in this slacks trying to think of something to say. And as if a light bulb went off for him. He frowned.

"Wait. Why are you here in Juliana's bedroom?"

Carson's jaw clenched.

"I came over here to talk to Juliana about my son."

"In her bedroom?" Rowan questioned. "It looks to me you were hiding."

"Look," Carson said.

Rowan peered at me and back and Carson. He pulled his hand out his pocket and rubbed the top of his head with his mouth slightly open.

"You two? I can't believe this. You've been sleeping with him too?" he asked with eyes that were judging me.

"Yes," I answered.

"Juliana," Carson blurted.

"What Carson? Rowan is no fool. The two of you got caught."

Both men expressions darkened. Rowan turned and walked back into the living space as Carson and I followed him.

"So now what?" I asked curiously.

"Rowan is going to stop seeing my daughter."

Rowan whirled around saying, "What?"

"That's right. I don't want no man, who can't be faithful, marrying my daughter."

"Are you being faithful pastor?" Rowan scoffed.

"You have nothing to do with that."

"Why don't I? I care for Mrs. Reid. How do you think she will feel if she found out you too were stepping out on her? At least I haven't said my vows yet."

"And you won't."

"Says who?"

"You better call this wedding off. I'm not having a two bit cheating punk breaking my daughter's heart."

"And you think me calling off our wedding will not break her heart."

"Better this than her finding out she married an impostor."

"Wow," Rowan said turning away.

"Look guys, both of you are wrong here. And both of you have a lot to lose if this ever comes out."

"Him more than me," Rowan added. "Isn't that right Pastor Reid. I wonder what the good people in

Greater Faith Baptist would think of the good reverend who can't be faithful to his wife."

"Don't threaten me son," Carson snarled.

"Then don't demand me to do something I'm not willing to do. From where I stand, it looks as though the both of us are walking out of here today with are tails tucked between our legs and our mouths shut," Rowan said.

Carson didn't disagree.

"Then that's it. What happened here today stays in this room? This is over."

"Is it? What about Aden?" Rowan asked.

Carson looked at me waiting for the answer to that question.

"I'm going to keep seeing Aden. We all need to go on like none of this ever happened, agreed."

Both of them said nothing, being the answer, I needed in order to move forward with what I wanted to do. Both had a lot to lose but me on the other hand, I had the upper hand. Actually, this couldn't have played out better for me. I had both men on the fence and it was nothing neither of them could do about it.

Amelia

Elaine decided to call me before I left the house with the idea of getting a pedicure before we had lunch and I surely agreed to this idea. There was nothing like getting pamper even if it was from the knee down. I needed something to help me release some of the tension that was building within me. Even though I was a pastor's wife, I was still human. I knew I was supposed to be the example but no one on this here earth was perfect. Not even me. Lord knows I've tried to maintain this image of Christianity, but it's been difficult. And right now, I knew I wasn't acting like I should, but I couldn't help it. The devil was bringing out all of his weaponry trying to attack me at all sides and I could feel myself slipping lower into my emotions and I didn't like it.

Elaine and I sat side by side in the comfortable leather chairs with the motors working our back muscles. Each of us laid our heads back and enjoyed the hot water bubbling between our toes.

"This feels wonderful," Elaine moaned with delight. "I'm so glad I thought of this."

"I'm glad you thought of this too."

"So how have things been? I haven't had a chance to catch up with you."

"Everything is good. Carson is better and Payton's wedding planning is coming along. But Aden?" I said sitting up to look at her.

"What's going on with him?"

"My son has decided to hook up with the church ho."

"Which one?"

This caused me to laugh before I asked, "What do you mean which one?"

"You've been sitting up in that first lady space too long. The church is full of Jezebels."

"The Jezebel I'm referring to is Juliana Simmons."

"Stop lying, Amelia? She's the Queen of sleeping around. I know my nephew isn't involved with that whore," Elaine spat.

"I wish this wasn't true."

"You mean big bootie Judy who's a major cutie who use to work down at Hooters."

"Okay Sir Mix Elaine."

"You caught my rhyming skills, huh," she said giggling.

"You are too old to be trying to spit any kind of rap."

"Look at the pot calling the kettle Mrs. Pastor's Wife. You know you should not be using words like ho, spit, and rap. You should have said promiscuous, talk, and sing the gospel," she said with an accent like she was having tea and crumpets in England.

I reached over and tapped her on the arm and she burst into laughter.

"You know we come from the same streets. We clubbed together. We drank together. We even puff, puff passed together. We've come a long way," Elaine said.

"I know. And just because I'm in the church, doesn't mean I still can't go back to my roots," I admitted.

Elaine looked at me with a side eye getting ready to respond but I interrupted her by saying, "I'm not talking about drinking and smoking."

She closed her mouth and smiled. I knew Elaine like the back of my hand.

"Oh, because I was getting ready to get happy. I haven't smoked in some years now, but I hear it's like riding a bike. I could use more than a pedicure to relax me right now."

As much as I could use a stiff drink and even some weed to relax me, that was not my life anymore.

I leaned my head back in defeat saying, "It's difficult being me."

"What does that supposed to mean? It's difficult being me too. I'm pretty sure everybody walking around thinks the same way. Especially these women working on my feet. How someone can love buffing people's feet is beyond me. I don't even like putting lotion on my own feet because I'm lazy. But I do it anyway, so I won't cut up my sheets or cut your bother up."

I burst into more laughter at this crazy girl. It was so good to laugh again.

"I didn't mean it like that, Elaine. I know everybody is going through something."

"I'm just saying, Amelia. From the outside looking in, your life looks magnificent. There are quite a few people who would love to take your place."

"That's one of my problems. If they are not coming for my husband, there are gunning for my son," I explained.

"The men in the church are checking you out too."

"I don't pay attention to them."

"I know you don't because you only have eyes for Carson."

"Which I should because he's my husband."

"There is nothing wrong with looking. It's the touching part that gets people in trouble," Elaine clarified.

"Can you imagine me looking at any other man besides my husband? Do you know what those noisy church ladies would say?"

"Forget them. Most of the noisy people minding everybody else business are unhappy with their own life. That's why they have time to meddle in everybody else's business."

"That may be true, but I don't know how much longer this church lady demeanor is going to hold up. Sometimes I feel like exploding, Elaine."

"Then explode. We are all allowed a moment to lose it."

"I'm scared if I do, I'm going to hurt somebody."

"I'll bail you out of jail."

"Elaine."

"I would," she asserted.

"I'm not trying to go to jail. What would it look like for a first lady to be behind bars?"

"It look like it look. If you ask me, I would think some could relate. It will show you are human just like everybody else."

"People don't see me as human. They see me as a representation of church, like I'm not supposed to have feelings. I have to drop everything I'm doing to help everyone and do everything with a smile to perfection."

"Who can do that? Even the ones complaining can't. If they ever got bold enough to confront me on how I should be acting I would tell them the only judgment I'm worried about it that of our God."

"You know I can do that, but I know it's going to be how I deliver it. I'm not in the correct spirit. I'm going to come off as angry."

"Which you would be."

"Yes but…"

"But nothing, Amelia. You put a lot of pressure on yourself."

"I know."

"You have to go with the flow of things and take it day by day, hour by hour if you have to or else you are going to drive yourself crazy."

"It hard not to worry. And Aden, my goodness, he's sent my anxiety level through the roof."

"You've raised him. There is nothing you can do about the decisions he's making. My nephew is young, and dumb and full of..."

"Don't say it Elaine," I said giving her the eye.

"I wasn't."

"Yes, you were."

"Okay I was. But let that boy do his grown man thing. You can't live his life for him either. You are having a hard time living your own."

"Ain't that the truth?"

"As for Carson, that man loves you. He's not going anywhere. You guys have been together forever. The life you have built has been done by the both of you."

"I know you are right, but I know my husband is a man, just like my son. What if some woman comes into the picture Carson can't resist?"

"Stop worrying about the what if's, Amelia. You got enough to worry about without making up scenarios to bring more added stresses to yourself. Oh, my goodness you are making me exhausted just listening to you. Let this stuff go."

"That's easier said than done," I responded.

"You and Carson's love for one another has endured so much. That man loves everything about you

115

including your dirty draws. I remember you telling me he use to pick up your dirty underwear to take a long whiff just because he loved your scent," she said shivering like it was the worst thing ever. "Ewh. Just thinking about that makes, me want to throw up in my mouth."

I looked at her in shock because she was disclosing too much of my information.

"Remind me not to tell you nothing personal again," I said.

"You think I forgot about that," Elaine said giggling.

"I can't believe you said it."

"Well it's true. Everything I'm saying to you is factual. Your marriage is rock solid. As for Aden, if you try to pull that boy away from that woman, all he's going to do is want to be with her more. I don't know what is with people wanting something they know they shouldn't have."

"It's been that way for centuries," I added.

"Act like you don't care and then eventually he will not care either."

Elaine was right. I never looked at this way. I was busy trying to control things driving myself crazy when I knew not all things were in my control anyway.

"You ready now," a young Japanese woman asked Elaine.

"Yes, you can start," she told her, and the young lady sat down in front of her on a stool. Another woman joined beside her to work on me. They were ready to get us out of these seats because a few people entered wanting a pedicure also.

I lifted my right foot up for the woman to begin and watched as the lady did the same to Elaine.

As she removed the bright red polish from my toes, I continued my conversation.

"Thank you, Elaine."

"For what?" she asked.

"For being my friend," I told her.

"Girl, you know we are more than friends. We are sisters for life. All I ever want for you is happiness," she said reaching out for my hand and I lovingly took it.

"I want the same for you too," I said smiling.

"Now, let's sit back, enjoy this pedicure and give whatever you are worried about over to God. Because if he can't fix it, no one can."

"Amen."

Skye

I knew Fatima was trying to help me catch my husband, but this didn't feel right. Yes, I needed proof of him cheating on me but was this the way to do it. Was she willing to help me because she wanting to swoop in and take Seth as her own. She did say she wasn't interested in anything further with him, but she could've been using reverse psychology on me to get what she wanted.

I wasn't expecting her call so soon. When I saw her name pop up on my cell, I hesitated. This was it. Today was going to be the day I was going to see for myself what Seth was doing.

"Hello," I answered.

"I can't talk long," she said in a low tone. "Seth is here with me now."

My heard dropped when she said this.

"My front door will be left unlock. Come right in. My bedroom is the last room on the right down the hallway. I will text you my address."

"Okay," was all I could say. And just like that the call ended.

When the navigation told me, you have reached your destination, I couldn't believe how close it was to my place of employment. I passed by this street leading to her home every day on my way to work. Her home was cute, nothing like what Seth and I acquired but for a starter home it was a charming brick style ranch with a paved driveway and a fence surrounding the back yard. Her lawn was beautifully manicured as colorful flowers and plush shrubs made her home appear more inviting.

I fixated on all of this to avoid the obvious. There in the driveway sat Seth's black Audi. He was parked right behind her silver Honda coupe like he lived here. He had to be comfortable enough with her if he pulled in like he paid bills here. Could he be paying bills here? It wasn't like I kept up with his money like that. As long as our bills got paid, I didn't worry about it.

Then I wondered how long had they been seeing each other. I never asked her. I was afraid of what it meant for our marriage because then I would have to face the reality that the amount of time they spent together could equal a substantial part of our marriage.

Water filled my eyes. I considered driving away. I could act like I never got the call from Fatima and take myself to the restaurant to meet, Camille.

Camille! I forgot all about her. I looked at the time on my cell phone and saw it was 1:43pm. We were supposed to meet at the Outback at 2:00pm. I searched through my log and found her number.

"Hello," she said happily.

"Hey, Camille. I'm calling to tell you I may not be able to make it."

"Why?" she asked.

"I got something I have to do."

"Then do it and come to the restaurant after," she suggested.

"I don't know how long it's going to take."

"I can wait for you. Besides, I'm starving, and I really looked forward to having me a glass of wine and a big huge T-Bone. So, do what you have to do and come on over. I'll wait."

I paused and didn't say anything, wondering after this confrontation, would I feel like doing anything at all.

"Skye, are you there?"

"I'm here."

"Girl, I told you I'm here if you need me."

120

Tears ran down my face when she said that. I wanted to tell her so bad what I was about to do but I was too ashamed. I couldn't admit I failed at this marriage.

"Skye," Camille called out. "Where are you? I'm coming to you."

"No, I'm good," I struggled to say.

"No, you are not. I can tell something is really wrong. Are you crying?"

"I'm okay, Camille."

"There you go, lying to me again."

"I'm good."

"Look, do what you go to do and then bring your behind to this restaurant. I'm going to be waiting for you. I will be disappointed if you don't show."

"I'm coming."

"Good. And plan to tell me what is going on with you. You got me worried."

Camille and I said our good-byes and hung up with one another. I gaped at the house, getting my courage up to exit my car.

When I turned the knob to enter Fatima's home, the scent of cinnamon greeted me like a grandmother's open arms. It reminded me of my childhood and how simpler life was then. Too bad this was not a simple act I was about to do. I slowly entered, taking in the space that surrounded me. Her living room was beautiful. Dark mahogany hardwood floors shimmered from the light shining through the plantation shutters. A white sofa with tangerine colored pillows sat across from a fireplace with a flat screen television over it. A white and yellow area rug anchored the space beautifully which seemed a lot larger than I expected. Everything looked so clean and neat. I didn't know why I expected different. She didn't seem like the type who would have such an elegant place. I loved things to be in order and it seemed like this was something Fatima and I had in common besides my husband.

I made my way down the hallway like she told me and looked for the last bedroom on the right. As I made my way, I took in her home and appreciated the lovely taste she had as each space was skillfully decked out with walls painted a monotone color, chrome picture frames, stainless steel appliances, and granite counter tops. I mean I could go on with how serene her home looked and felt.

When I got close to the bedroom door she told me to come to, I paused. Preparing myself for what I was about to see, a drew in a breath. The door was slightly ajar. I lifted my hand to push the door open and noticed my hand was trembling with the anticipation. Lowering my hand and shook it some, trying to gather the strength to do this. Was I ready? I thought I was but who could ever get ready for their world to be torn apart like this.

Null and Void

"Ooohhh, that feels good," I heard a voice say.

My gut wrenched with pain as I recognized that it was Seth's voice I was hearing. I fell back against the wall for fear of falling to my knees in devastation.

"Yes baby, like that," he said, and the anxiety of my marriage being ruined was quickly replaced with the rage.

I stepped forward, pushed the door open until I was looking into the room. There was Seth lying on his back while this…..this…this thick sister pleasuring my husband orally. I didn't know if I was shocking to see him being pleasured by another woman or the fact he was being pleasured by a plus size woman. Her massive behind was up in the air towards me as he gripped her head as she bobbed up and down on his manhood. He never noticed me. How could he, when he had his eyes closed shut with a handful of her long hair enjoying being serviced?

For some reason, I didn't speak. I watched to see how long it was going to take for either of them to notice me. I decided to reach in my pocket and pull out my cell phone. I held my cell in the air and held the button down to the camera snapping numerous pictures. The flash let both of them know someone was watching and when she released herself long enough to notice me, Seth opened his eyes wondering why she'd stopped.

Her eyes directed him to look in my direction. He turned to see me standing in the doorway.

123

"What tha-," he said pushing Fatima to the side and jumping to his feet covering himself with his hand. "Skye, baby, what are you doing here?"

"I like your nerve. You're asking me what I'm doing here. What are you doing here?"

"I'm...I'm...I'm..."

"Spit it out," I yelled snapping more pictures. He held his hand up trying to block the flash and keep his privates from showing. "What are you doing here, Seth?"

"Baby, look. I can explain," he said picking up his pants off the floor and holding them in front of him like I hadn't seen his private parts before. His was the very first one I'd seen, and I thought had the pleasure of having it all to myself once we said our vows, but I was mistaken.

"Explain what, how you got your rod stuffed down her throat."

Seth looked at Fatima who was sitting on the crumpled sheets on the bed. She didn't have a care in the world.

"I asked you if you were cheating on me and you told me no. Do you remember?" I asked Seth.

"Yes."

"You had me thinking I was crazy. You laid me out and wouldn't even talk to me for having the audacity to accuse you of such a thing. And look at you. You standing here butt naked. So, am I crazy now, Seth? Or are you going to find a way to spin this to make me feel like I'm the one whose wrong here?"

Tears were streaming down my cheeks. I knew my intuition was right all along, but I didn't want to believe it. I wanted to trust my husband was being faithful to me and wouldn't do anything to jeopardize our marriage. I thought something was wrong with me for having those thoughts but now I knew my gut was accurate.

"Okay, you got me," Seth said dropping his pants as he stood before the both of us with nothing on. "Now what?" he asked crossing his arms across his chest cockily like he didn't care he'd been caught.

"What now? You are asking me what now."

"Yes," he said callously. "Are you leaving me? Are we getting a divorce, what?"

"Why are you being so cold?" I asked.

"Look, Skye, I don't know what you want from me. You got what you wanted. You caught me in a lie. Now it's time for you to figure out exactly what the next move should be."

"I can't believe you. You are not going to try to defend yourself."

"And say what?" he hunched his shoulders.

"Explain to me why you did this. At least show an ounce of compassion about saving our marriage."

"Look at where you are, Skye. You are standing in the house of the woman I've been sleeping with for some time now. It's obvious I'm not happy in our marriage if I'm here with her."

"Do you even want to be in this marriage?" I asked fearfully, not sure if I wanted to hear his answer since it seemed like he didn't care.

"I'm not sure."

I almost crumpled to the floor where I stood. I did stumble back but manage to keep myself upright.

"You are not sure?" I asked nodding dejectedly.

"I'm sorry you had to find out like this."

"Are you?" I asked him.

He didn't respond, which let me know he wasn't. He was telling me what he thought I wanted to hear.

"I'm going to leave now. I have a lunch date with Camille."

Seth snickered and said, "So that's it. You are just going to leave just like that?"

"What else am I supposed to do?" I asked.

"How about scream, fight, yell, or even throw something at me for that matter. You just saw my private in her mouth," he said pointing to Fatima, "and all you can say is I'm leaving to go have lunch?"

"I can't do this with you now."

"So, when is a good time, Skye, when we get home? Or how about next week. You see, that's your problem. You never want to deal with what's in front of you. You are so weak."

His words hurt me to my core. I knew I was a bit timid but the word weak sounded so much worst coming from him.

"You act like you didn't know I was like this, Seth. I've never been a confrontational person."

"I did but now I'm tired of it."

"So, it would have made you happy to bash you over the head with something?"

"At least I would have known you cared and had some other type of emotion other than being a stuck up coward."

"What?" I said breathlessly.

"Get a backbone and stand up for yourself. No one wants a weak minded individual."

"So why did you marry me? I haven't shown you anything different."

"I don't know. I've been asking myself that question for months now."

I couldn't take any more of his insults. I observed Fatima who sat patiently on the bed while Seth and I carried on our conversation. I didn't like the fact we did this in front of her. But she probably knew more about my marriage than I did. Especially since he was standing here telling me what he didn't like about me. I'm pretty sure he'd told her that already.

"We will talk later," I said turning to walk away.

I could hear him talking to her as I made my way down the hallway.

"You see what I'm saying, weak. If you would have caught me doing this, Fatima, what would you have done?"

"I would have tried to kill you," I could hear her say.

But that wasn't me. I was not the violent type. I felt like everything could be discussed in order to resolve issues. Evidently, Seth wanted something different from me but didn't have the balls to disclose this to me. I didn't know what my next move was going to be.

As soon as I stepped foot out that woman's door, I broke down sobbing. I couldn't wait to get to my car just, so I could sit for a moment and catch my breath. I didn't know what else to do because I was truly shattered. My marriage was over. Just like that, Seth was willing to throw away what we'd built for some sex. I felt like an utter failure. When I said my vows to this man, I meant it. I saved myself for this man for goodness sake because I thought he was my soul mate till death do us part. Was I a fool to trust in him? Did I want to get married so bad that I over looked all the signs that we may not work. Did I really know Seth at all?

Skye

When I walked into the restaurant, I saw Camille sitting in our usual spot located in the middle of the restaurant. Generally, this was okay with me but with my red puffy eyes and runny nose, I wanted to be seated in a corner where no one could see the results of my breakdown. I could have reapplied my makeup, but I didn't have the energy, which was why I looked like a hot mess walking up in here.

"Sorry I'm late," I said sitting down hastily hoping Camille wouldn't notice my emotional appearance.

"What is wrong with you?"

I shook my head not able to speak. Those words were like a signal for another round of tears to stream down my cheeks. As hard as I struggled against the release of pressure, as soon as I looked into Camille's face, I lost my battle. I quickly picked up the napkin surrounding the silverware and wiped my fallen tears away. This was why I wanted to sit in a corner. I didn't want anyone to notice me losing it like this.

"Skye, we can leave if you want. Let's get this food to go and go back to your place."

"I can't go home right now," I sniffled.

"Okay then. We can go to my house," she suggested. "You okay with that?"

I nodded, using the cloth napkin to dab at my tears.

Camille waved her hand summoning the waiter. Once he was at our table she asked, "Can you please take our order and make it to go?"

The waiter looked at me and nodded with understanding. Even a stranger showed some sympathy for me and my own husband didn't to comfort me. He took our orders and left to quickly put them in.

"Thank you, Camille. I'm sorry for this."

"You don't have to thank me or apologize. I don't want anyone all up in your business," she said looking at a couple at the table next to us cutting their eye our way.

"Excuse me. Do you see something over here you like?" Camille barked.

The woman, who appeared to be in her late sixties, scoffed as she turned away abruptly. Her husband on the other hand smiled like he wanted to answer Camille's questions with a yes. As old as he was, he didn't look like he could do anything for either of us but have a heart attack.

When we arrived at Camille's place, we dropped our bags of food on her coffee table in the living room. I was in no mood to eat. I couldn't get the image of Fatima pleasing my husband out of my head. I wanted to kick myself for agreeing to her suggestion. Granted, it was something I needed to found out but not like I found it.

Camille disappeared into her kitchen and returned with a bottle of Moscato and two wine glasses.

"I figured we needed this," she said, sitting down beside me on the sofa.

After pouring us a gracious amount of the wine, she took a long sip before she started speaking.

"Please tell me what's wrong with you, Skye. You got me worried."

"I can do better than tell you."

I reached into my purse and pulled out my cell phone. I clicked to my photos and found the pictures of Seth with his side piece and handed Camille my phone.

Her mouth dropped open.

"You have got to be kidding me," she uttered.

I sipped my wine watching her reaction.

"This can't be... I know this ain't... Was she... Wait a... I can't..." she kept pausing, pointing to my phone, then at me for acknowledgment. She never did finish a full sentence as she scanned through the photos.

"Okay," she finally relented handing me my phone. "That's too much. So that's what had you so upset?"

I nodded again, taking another long sip of the wine.

"Home girl was going to town wasn't she?"

Camille noticed the troubled expression on my face and said, "I'm sorry. I didn't mean to say that."

"It's okay. The disturbing scene is branded in my mind and is being replayed over and over again in high definition."

"Not only high definition. Girl, you got the 3D version without the special glasses. Did he explain himself?" she asked.

"He said it was because I was weak?"

"Weak?" Camille said sourly. I thought her eyes were going to pop out of her head they were stretched so wide.

"Yep. He was even mad I didn't tear things up, yell, scream and bust him in the head with something when I found him with her."

"Why didn't you?" Camille asked with a grimace. "You are a woman who just caught her husband with another woman. This situation warrants a beat down. You're better than me because I would have tried to cut off that very thing that caused him to cheat and that's what's dangling between his legs."

"What would that solve?" I asked. "All you are going to do is land yourself in jail."

"That's fine. But every time he got ready to go to the bathroom or be intimate with a woman, he would have no choice but to think about me and why he's missing that body part. Besides, once I get arrested, I would plead not guilty due to severe emotional and mental defect. Catching your husband with some woman is enough to push anybody over the edge. I don't understand how you are holding up as well as you are. If I was you, I would be home cutting up his clothes and roasting some hot dogs over them once I sat his things on fire."

"Camille," I said in shock.

"He would find me chilling with my feet up next to the bonfire I created using his things to enjoy a nice barbecued dog with mustard."

Laughing, I said, "You are crazy."

"I'm for real. A few things I don't like played with," she said sitting her glass down. "Don't play with my food. Don't play with my money. Don't disrespect my parents. And don't break my heart," she said holding up four fingers as she counted out those things. "If you mess with any of those things, I will reveal a side of me that could get me featured on an episode of *Snapped*."

I giggled at my friend. It felt good to laugh even though my life was falling apart.

"And if I had children, they would be on that list also."

"I wish I was more like you," I admitted.

Camille picked up her drink and took a sip before asking, "You can be. I would be happy to teach a class on how to whoop that…"

"Camille," I stopped her.

"I forget you don't like all that cursing and stuff. I was doing well up to this point, but this got me hot."

"It's okay."

"What's your next move?" she asked taking another sip.

"I don't know."

"Are you filing for a divorce?"

"I don't want to," I said undoubtedly.

"Why not?"

"Because when I got married it was for life. I promised God this."

"You don't think God can see the devil at work here. You married him. Your husband has committed several sins and one of them is a Commandment. *Thou shalt not commit adultery.*"

"But we all sin. Romans 3:23 says *For all have sinned, and come short of the glory of God;*"

"Leviticus 20:10 says *If there is a man who commits adultery with another man's wife, one who commits adultery with his friend's wife, the adulterer and the adulteress shall surely be put to death.* That means you need to kill him."

"No, it doesn't," I corrected her. "There you go turning around a scripture to make it fit what you want."

"What else does it mean?"

"I can't punish him. He'll we get what's coming to him."

"It still doesn't negate the fact you need to leave him. If you say, then he's going to continue to do it because it's going to seem like you cool with it."

"I don't know if I can."

"Does that man love you enough to make your marriage work?"

Her question caused me to pause. I didn't know the answer to that and to me that was sad. If she would have asked me this yesterday, I would have said yes. But today, things were turned upside down. Maybe if Seth would have reacted differently, I would think he wanted our marriage to work. But I knew as soon as I left his mistresses home, he probably crawled back in the bed with her to finish what they started. The thought of that almost made me break down again.

"Camille, I don't know much of anything anymore. I can't figure out what my next move is."

"A relationship can't work with one person committed to it. That love conquers all is a bunch of lies because if the person you are trying to love doesn't value the gift of what you are offering, then you're wasting unnecessary energy on a dead situation."

That impacted me. A dead situation. As much as I wanted to feel my marriage could be saved, I knew our marriage was just that, dead. And Seth was responsible for killing it. I still wasn't sure what I was going to do next but one this if for sure, I was going to have to go to God with this one hoping he give me clarity on what to do and soon.

Amelia

Carson called and told me he was running late for
dinner because he was called to the hospital because one
of the church members was admitted for having a stroke.
The family wanted him to pray over their loved one
during this tough time.

I knew this was part of Carson's calling but
sometimes I wanted him to choose our home before he
chose everyone else. I know his title as pastor called for
him to do all of these things, but it seemed to be
happening more often than not. When my husband had
pneumonia, I had to admit I was happy about it. He
couldn't do anything but sit and get well. He couldn't
attend board meetings or be the guest preacher at
surrounding churches. And he couldn't visit the sick and
shut in. It was just him and I and it was great. It would
have been perfect if he sister Dee Dee wasn't around.

Carson was probably glad he got the call this
evening, so he wouldn't have to meet with his sister to

inform her she needed to pack her belongings and get out of our house. I didn't mean any harm but whatever hour he got in tonight, he was still going to tell Dee Dee because I was sick and tired of having her around.

Speak of the devil and they appear. Dee Dee came walking into the kitchen with her hair and nails freshly done like she had a job. She had on another outfit I hadn't seen before. She wore a pair of diamond printed black and white leggings with a yellow sleeveless ruffled chiffon blouse. The outfit actually looked cute on her even though she was a fluffy woman. Dee Dee always knew how to carry the extra weight she had. For somebody with no job and no money, she always seemed to find money to look her best.

All I could think about was this could be the money she could be saving to put down on her own place. But she wasn't thinking about doing that because she was comfortable. Comfortable people always overstayed their welcome. How they couldn't see being a freeloader was a problem was beyond me.

"You got it smelling amazing up in here. What you cooking?"

"Food," I said tartly.

"I know that silly but what food. Did you make your roast? I love your pot roast. I don't know what you do but it's my favorite."

"No. I made pork chops smothered in gravy with mash potatoes and cabbage."

"Ummmm that sounds wonderful. We can we eat."

With my back turned to her as I stood at the stove stirring the cabbage, I rolled my eyes. I took in a deep breath trying to tolerate this woman.

"Did you hear me, Amelia? When can we eat?"

"Yes, I heard you, Dee Dee. You can eat in a bit."

"Are we waiting for Carson?" she asked.

"No. He's going to be home late."

"Again?"

I didn't bother to respond. She knew if Carson wasn't home by seven, he was running late. This was the same conversation we had practically every day. She would smell the food, come sniffing around when she thought it was close to being done. This got on my last nerve.

"My brother really needs to slow down. That's why he got sick in the first place because he's doing too much."

I kept quiet.

"I hope he gets here soon because I really need to talk to him about this car I want. I know he told me I don't need it, but I really do want it."

A car. Did she just say she wanted a car? She was supposed to be trying to get her own place. That was it. I was done with her. I had to say something.

I whipped around glaring at her in annoyance.

"Why do you need to talk to Carson?"

"Because I'm going to need his help to get it," she answered.

"Why can't you get a job and buy your own car, Dee Dee?"

My tone was firm and a bit harsh but I didn't care. I was tired of this grown woman acting like a child and not a responsible adult.

"Why you getting your panties in a bunch about?" she frowned.

"I'm like this because of you," I pointed to her.

"What have I done?"

"That's just it. You haven't done anything. You don't do anything. All you do is sit around this house likes it's yours. You are eating up the food we buy and watching the cable we pay for like you are our child. And let's not forget about the cell phone bill we are paying for also."

"I'm having some financial issues."

"Yet, you are standing here in a new outfit, your hair and your nails done."

"What? I can't treat myself once in a while."

"You treat yourself all the time. How about treating yourself to a place of your own," replying curtly.

"Look, jobs are scarce around here. I've tried to find work."

"Where?" I asked.

"I've applied for multiple receptionist jobs. I've applied to be an accountant and a hairstylist."

I burst into laughter saying, "Do you have experience with any of those positions?"

"No, but it's what I want to do."

"Want and need are two different things. You need to find something that's going to get you where you need to be until you can get trained and find something that you want."

"You expect me to flip burgers?"

"I expect you do whatever it takes to get you out of my house," I asserted.

"I can't believe you feel this way."

I wanted to scream at this ignorant woman who never got it. I wanted to shake some common sense in her to see she's a moocher.

"Carson better hurry up and get here," I mumbled.

"Why do you say that?" she asked.

"Because he doesn't want to talk to you about getting out of here."

"Maybe he doesn't want me to leave. Maybe, he doesn't mind helping me during my time of need."

"How long do you expect help, Dee Dee?"

"I don't know."

"You've been here for almost a year. I know it's hard out here and it takes time for someone to get on their feet, but you are not even trying. The money you using to make yourself look fabulous and going to dinners and parties could've been used to find your own place by now. So, since Carson is not here to tell you this, I'm letting you know it's time for you to go."

"What?" she sputtered.

"You heard me. You have until the end of the week to get out of our house."

Dee Dee's happy go lucky expression quickly changed to one of befuddlement.

"Are you serious?"

"Yes I am. I tried to give you a chance by letting you stay with us but it's clear you are taking advantage of us."

Dee Dee was mute for the first time in a long while. This woman's mouth ran a mile a minute and now she looked around like she was too flabbergasted to know what to say. When she woke up this morning, she didn't expect this. She thought she was going to continue to ride this gravy boat, but she was being thrown off. It would have been different if we saw her making an effort to better herself but wasn't. She clearly wasn't trying to leave but now she had no choice. This conversation should have happened a long time ago, but I loved my husband enough to allow this ungrateful house guest to stay longer than her she was welcome to. Not anymore.

"Where am I going to go?"

"I don't know. Maybe you can find an apartment. Like Carson said, we will help you with your deposit and first month's rent. But after that, you are on your own."

"Y'all can't do this to me," she retorted.

"Why can't we?" I asked.

"You have to give me more than a few days' notice."

"Says who?"

"Says the state of Virginia. Amelia, I may look stupid but I'm far from it. By law you have to give me thirty days."

I couldn't believe this woman knew this. And it angered me that she did. She didn't know how to work. She didn't know how to live on her own and take care of herself, but she knew this. I guess when you've been evicted several times, she knew her rights. Getting over was a way of life for her and she'd entrapped us into her usury. Isn't this like freeloaders?

"I want you out by Sunday," I stressed. "And I'm asking you nicely."

She took a couple of steps in my direction and said, "And I told you I have thirty days. If you keep pushing me, I will stay until the court tells me I have to leave. And please know I do know that could be up to ninety days."

I nodded angrily.

"Okay. You want your thirty days, then you can have them."

"That's what I thought. And since you been rude about this, I might take the ninety days anyway," she said confidently.

"You can try."

"Oh, I don't have to try."

My heart thudded in my chest from anger as heat rose within me.

"I'm going to tell you like this, Dee Dee. If you stay here for the thirty days or as you say the ninety days, you will not get a dime from us in helping you find a place. And if you, keep it up, you will never see a dime we make ever in this lifetime."

"You can't do that," she exclaimed. "Carson will not go for this."

"Oh, he will. Trust me, because we've already discussed this. So you either leave by Sunday with help from us or you can stay longer and leave here with what you came with."

Dee Dee snarled at me.

"I never liked your stuck-up behind."

"That's fine. I never liked your leeching behind either."

"I don't know what my brother ever saw in you. But it's okay. I guarantee you I will get the last laugh," she said stepping back with a smirk.

I wondered what her smirk was about, but I didn't care because she was getting out my face.

"I'm still going to have this house. I'm still going to have my assets and you will still be a person who uses people to get what she wants," I responded.

Dee Dee giggled.

"The mighty will fall. Trust and believe that," she said as she turned and walked out of the room singing a gospel tune.

Amelia

Carson didn't get home until after nine. I was sitting in the living room watching *"Mary Mary"* on WE TV when he came into the room. With my sweats and a tee one, I was curled up on the sofa with my favorite black fleece throw. I was minutes away from dozing off. It seemed like the older I got, the sooner I wanted to go to sleep. The only reason why I was in the living room and not in my bed was because I wanted to get to Carson first before his sister got to him.

"Hey, baby," he greeted, coming over to me and giving me a kiss.

"Hey yourself."

He plopped down next to me and leaned his head back to loosen his tie to remove it from around his neck.

"I know you are tired."

"I am."

"How is Sister Mable?" I asked.

"She's unconscious but the doctors are hopeful she will come through this like a champ."

"Look at God."

"Isn't he marvelous?" Carson smiled.

"Yes, he his. I know her family was distraught."

"Amazingly, they all were holding up pretty good."

"Even her son, Jeremy? That boy is some kind of crazy of his mother."

"He wasn't there."

I looked at him with confusion.

"Why?" I asked.

"Unfortunately, Jeremy is locked up."

"For what?"

"Being in the wrong place at the wrong time. He was with some guys who tried to rob, and convenience store and you know when they arrest one…"

"...They arrest them all."

"Exactly. His sister went to the jail to tell him about his mother."

"Hopefully this wasn't what sent his mother to the hospital in the first place," I said wondering did this woman have a stroke due to her broken heart of this boy.

"I don't know, honey. All I know is I'm glad she's going to be find and I'm home sitting next to you."

He placed a comforting hand on my leg looking at me lovingly.

"I fixed your plate. It's in the microwave."

"Thank you, baby," he said sitting up to get up.

I grabbed his arm to stop him saying, "Before you go, I need to talk to you about something."

"Okay honey," he said.

He leaned back again and before I had a chance to say one word, his sister entered the room.

"I can't believe you would do your own sister like this," Dee Dee spat.

"What are you talking about?" Carson asked looking at her with a frown.

"I told Dee Dee she has until Sunday to move out," I said. "I was going to tell you, but your sister didn't give me a chance."

I knew this was the last thing he wanted to deal with when he got home, which was why I didn't spring this on him as soon as he got in. If I would've known his sister was waiting in the wings to pounce on him, I would have explained what happened before he got blindsided.

"Is this true, Carson? Do you want me to move out?" Dee Dee asked him.

Carson hesitated, looking between the woman whom he was married to and the woman who carried the same DNA as him.

"Is it true, Carson?" she asked again, this time with more of a raised voice.

"Yes. It's true," he finally admitted.

"Are you sure this is how you want to carry things?"

She was talking like we owed her something and as far as I knew, we didn't owe her anything.

"Dee Dee, we've given you plenty of time to get it together, don't you think?"

"No."

"Well, we have. I know my wife told you we will help you as much as we can."

"Only if I'm out by Sunday."

Carson cast a gaze my way and I nodded.

Turning his attention back to his sisters he said, "Yes, this is true."

I sat back looking at her like I told you so. My husband was going to stick by my side. I wanted to act like I was five and do a happy dance in her face, but I maintained.

Dee Dee shook her head in disbelief.

"Okay. I will be out of your home by Sunday."

I wanted to say good, but I wasn't trying to add gas to the flames.

"You know I love you, Dee Dee. But I also love my wife."

"You have a funny way of showing it."

"Haven't I shown it to you by allowing you to stay here? I've taken care of you for quite some time, more than even my wife is aware of."

What did he mean by that I thought?

"I appreciate all you have done for me, Carson, but you didn't have to do me like this. You could've sat me down and talked with me about this instead of letting your wife tell me how you guys felt. I thought we were closer than that."

"We are. I was supposed to talk to you, but I've been busy. Don't blame her because it's my fault."

"I'm blaming her and I'm blaming you too. We've been through too much together for you to allow her to come between us. We've lost our parents. We've lost our brother. We are all we got. It was you and me before she came along."

"You act like I've stopping loving you, sis."

"Haven't you. You're kicking me out."

"I'm kicking you out because I love you. How I've been helping you is actually hindering you. What if something happens to me? Who's going to help you then?"

Dee Dee looked my way, but I didn't say anything. And neither did she. I wasn't about to say I was.

"That's why I'm doing this, so you can learn to stand on your own two feet. I can't keep taking care of you. You are a grown woman. You moving out is not going to change our relation as siblings and the fact I love you," Carson explained.

"Me moving out is not what hurts, Carson. It's how this all transpired. You have always come to me with everything. And I mean everything," she said giving him a look that puzzled me.

It didn't go unnoticed that Carson shifted uneasy.

"But it's okay. I'm going to leave you and your wife to live your happy life. Like I said earlier, I will be out of your hair by Sunday."

"I'm still here for you. As soon as you find a place, let me know," Carson reiterated.

She said nothing as she exited the room. The moocher was moving out and I was happy I was finally going to get my house back to myself. Still, my spirit was troubled. Here I was thinking it had to do with my son, but could it have to do with Dee Dee or my husband for that matter?

Skye

When Seth walked through the door leading from the garage, I glanced over at the clock on the stove to see it was 11:23 pm. Instead of coming home after our incident, he decided to stay out later than he usually did. I guess he figured he might as well since everything was out in the open. I sat at the kitchen table with my legs crossed and my foot bouncing in the air in irritation.

"What is this?" Seth asked with a grimace.

"Sit down son," his mother said to him as she sat at the table with me.

That's right, I called his mother. I know this looked like I was trying to get him in trouble with his mother but if he didn't want to talk to me, then I brought somebody here who I knew he had no other choice but to speak with. It may have been wrong to get her involved, but I was willing to do whatever it took to make this marriage work.

Seth defied his mother and said, "I'll stand." He leaned against the kitchen counter and crossed his arms in defense.

"I said sit down," she repeated with more sternness in her voice. Without uttering another word, he did as she said.

Ms. Wanda may have been a tiny little thing standing only about five feet, but she meant business. She was one of them mothers that when they gave you one look, you knew what time it was. That's why didn't understand why Seth even thought to try her. He may have been grown but Ms. Wanda wouldn't hesitate putting her hands on her grown son.

She was a very attractive woman and didn't look sixty two at all. Most people thought she was in her forties. Every man she'd ever dated since Seth's father passed away has been younger than she was. The youngest guy she'd ever dated was twenty nine years old and she ended up dumping him because he wasn't fun enough for her. Can you believe that? She had more energy than a twenty nine year old.

I loved his mother dearly. We'd always had a wonderful relationship, which was why she was the one I turned to regarding this situation. If anybody was a cheerleader for this relationship, it was definitely her.

"Mom, I know Skye didn't call you over here to discuss our problems?" he asked casting me a burning gaze.

"She needed someone to talk to and since you weren't here, she called me."

"How convenient?" Seth said rolling his eyes.

"Why are you coming up in this house at this hour, Seth? We called you several times and you never picked up."

"I was busy."

"Busy doing what, screwing that woman she caught you with earlier today?" his mother asked.

Seth shot daggers my way again. I leaned back in my chair wishing I couldn't feel the hatred rising from him.

"Don't look at her like that. I'm talking to you," Ms. Wanda said.

"Mom, with all due respect, I don't want to talk to you about anything concerning what's going on in this house."

"Then tell me what happen at that other woman's house, since you don't want to talk about what's happening in this one?" his mother asked smartly.

I wanted to chuckle at her clever way of switching it around on him.

"What? Do you want details on how I seduced her?" he smarted back.

"First of all, you better check your tone before you be picking yourself off the floor. I don't know who you think you are talking to but you better watch what you say and how you say things to me. You got me?" she admonished.

"Yes, ma'am."

"I don't care who you're screwing but you better not ever in your life disrespect me like this again, Seth Anthony."

When Ms. Wanda got going, it was hard to get her to come back down from her anger. Calling Seth by his first and middle name was a sure sign she was ticked off. My husband dropped his head in shame. It was obvious where Seth got his rage from. This was the third time I'd ever been witness to his mother making someone feel like they needed to go crawl in a hole and hide. Lucky for me, I'd never been on the receiving end of her wrath.

"Smarting off to me. You've fell and bumped your head," she fussed.

"Mom, I'm sorry for disrespecting you but…"

"But. Apologies don't suppose to have buts, Seth. That cancels everything out you saying, and I don't think you want to do that with me."

"Mom, can I please talk?" he asked sincerely.

"If you can talk with some sense, you sure can," she gave him permission.

"I didn't mean to direct my anger at you," he said glaring at me to say his anger was supposed to be for me. "This is our issue, which should have been handled here in our home between me and Skye. She never should have involved you or Fatima for that matter."

"Fatima got herself involved when she called to tell me she was sleeping with you," I finally interjected. "How else do you think I knew when and where to catch your cheating behind? But you mad at me. What did I do wrong in this situation?" I asked.

"I guess nothing, Skye," he said cynically.

"Don't brush this off, Seth. Did Fatima tell you she's the one responsible for all of this?"

"She told me."

"But you are mad at me and stayed to chill with her. I'm the one you are married to," I said heatedly.

His eyes were heavy with irritation as he glowered at me.

"Son, instead of resolving your issues with your wife, you went outside your marriage to sleep with another woman and that's not how you handle your problems," Ms. Wanda said.

"You are right, mom but I'm not happy in this marriage."

"Did you tell Skye this?" his mom asked.

"She knew I wasn't happy," he assumed.

"Did you tell her?" Ms. Wanda asked again. "Did you break it down like you are doing with me now?"

"No Ma'am."

"That's where you went wrong first. You should have discussed your feelings with your wife. As you can see by your actions, you've created a bigger mess of things."

"I know," he agreed.

"You are mad at Skye for something you did wrong and that doesn't make any sense to me."

Seth paused, looking into his mother's brown eyes.

"Do you love her, son?"

"Love who?"

"Skye?" his mother with a frown.

Taking longer than I would have liked, he finally said, "Not like I love Fatima."

His revelation caused the earth to stop spinning for me. You could hear a pin drop in this moment of confession. His mother cast a gaze my way to see how I was dealing with his answer and all I tried to do was keep it together. I don't think I was breathing. All I could do was look at my husband with a wounded expression because I was truly shattered.

"You love her more than you love me?" I asked weakly, almost whispering the words to him.

"Yes," he admitted.

He lifted his chin up slightly like he was proud to admit how he felt about her. I'd been with this man for three years and I'd never seem him look like this for me.

"But…but…I thought you loved me?"

"I did, Skye…"

"Did? When did that change?" I asked.

"I can't give you a specific time."

"Guess?" I yelled.

"I don't know. Maybe eight months."

"Eight months?" I questioned.

"I'm sorry you had to find out like this but I'm glad it's finally out."

"Why, so you can be with Fatima?" I asked.

"Yes," he answered coldly.

Out the corner of my eye I could see Ms. Wanda shaking her head in disbelief. She reached across the table and took Seth's right hand into hers.

"Baby, I thought you cared for Skye."

"I do, Mom, but not like a husband does for his wife."

"Did you love me when you married me?" I managed to ask.

"Yes, but it was a different kind of love," he admitted.

"Different how?" I asked.

"I feel like I didn't know what true love was until I met Fatima. I cared for you Skye and yes, I even loved you, but I don't think it's the love you need from me."

"Then why did you marry me if you weren't sure?" I asked loudly.

"You really want the answer to that?" he asked.

"I'm asking aren't I," I belted.

"I married you, so I could sleep with me."

"Seth Anthony Holden," Ms. Wanda blurted gripping his hand.

"It's the truth, Ma. Skye was a virgin and didn't want to have sex until we were married. I felt like I'd spent all this time in this relationship with you, that I at least should sample the goods."

"Honey, Skye is not some hors d'oeuvres you try and if you don't like it, you spit it out," he mother said. "You are basically admitting to marrying her under false pretenses."

"Mom, I told you I wasn't sure, but you told me I had wedding jitters and every man gets those before saying his vows. I tried to tell Skye too but again, y'all thought I was nervous about the wedding. So, I went through with it."

"If I would have known this, I would have called off the wedding, Seth," I said gloomily.

"This is what you wanted. Y'all wanted me to speak my truth and here it is. I'm happy everything is out in the open. This way I can move on with my life," he explained.

"Move on," I muttered.

Ms. Wanda said, "Seth, maybe you guys need to go to counseling. Pastor Reid would be more than happy to help you two through this time of trouble."

"Mom, that's just it. There is no helping us anymore. I'm done," he said with finality.

"Just like that you are ready to leave me," I uttered gloomily.

"Yes," Seth said.

"Look me in my eyes and tell me you don't love me anymore and that you want to end our marriage," I demanded, thinking there was no way he could do this. There was no way our relationship, all this time, has been a farce. If he was deadest on breaking my heart, then he had to look me in my eyes and tell me.

Seth hesitated, staring at his mother. She nodded to him. He turned to look at me. I wanted him to see the pain in my face. I want him to take in the tears now streaming down my cheeks. I gave myself to this man. I saved myself for this man and he used me.

I trembled like a leaf on a tree being tossed around by unbridled wind. I was fearful he could do this. If he could look me dead in my eyes and tell me he doesn't want to be with me anymore, then he was being real with me.

"Skye," he said dropping his head in shame.

"Look me in my eyes and tell me you don't love me, and you want this marriage to end," I demanded again, knowing in his hesitation, he couldn't.

I was not about to let him be a coward about this. He was bold enough to cheat. Then he was going to be man enough to tell me to my face.

Seth paused for a long moment and I knew this meant he had to care for me, if not love me still.

"Admit it, Seth. You didn't mean what you said. You do love me," I reminded him.

My husband lifted his head, his brown eyes connecting with mine. He leaned forward with elbows to his knees and hands clenched together.

"Skye, I don't love you anymore and I want a divorce."

Juliana

Aden and I panted as we looked up towards the ceiling. A sheen of thin sweat coating our bodies as we relished in the afterglow of our encounter. I wished he was Carson and not this cheap knock off of his father, but I had to do whatever it took to get closer to him. And if being with Carson's son was what I had to do, then so be it. I was in love with him. I wanted Carson all to myself, but he refused to be with me because of that wife of his. If he was happy from the start, he wouldn't have gotten involved with me. Rowan only came in the picture when I realized I couldn't wait on Carson to make his mind up. Who knew he could turn out to be Carson's future son in law?

"Penny for your thoughts," Aden asked turning to his side to face me.

"I'm thinking about you," I lied. It sicken me to say that or anything else. I didn't feel like conversation with him. I wanted him to put his clothes on and leave so I could finish myself off since he couldn't satisfy me.

"Really?" he asked with raised brows looking elated.

"Yes. I'm wondering what we are doing."

"You don't know what we finished doing?" he questioned with a chuckle.

Playfully swinging at him I said, "I know that silly but I'm wondering what we are doing. Am I just a play thing to you? Are you using me or are you feeling me?"

"Where is this coming from?"

"It's coming from a place of hurt. I know you've heard about my reputation but what people don't know is that I'm not a whore. I just happened to be a woman who falls quick and easy for men only to get hurt in the end."

Aden gazed at me with a small smile. He leaned down and kissed my bare shoulder.

"We can be whatever you want us to be."

"Come on, Aden. I'm not trying to make a man be somewhere he doesn't. Why can't men tell you how they feel? Why is it always the woman who has to step up about her feelings and put a definition on things?"

"Baby, please don't get upset."

It was easy for me to get this way because the person I was referring to was Carson. I was tired of getting hurt and being used over and over again. I wanted love, not necessarily from Aden but from Carson.

Aden was a means to a happy ending for me. The closer I got to Aden, the closer I got to Carson.

"So, you not going to say anything else," Aden asked.

I shook my head in defiance.

"What if I told you, I love you?" Aden stated.

"Would it be true because those are words you can't just throw around?" I said.

"I don't play around with those words. If I say them, I mean them."

With a timid smile, I asked, "Are you saying you love me?"

"Yes, I do. And if you would have me as your man, I promise I will do my best to make you the happiest woman ever."

The look in Aden's eyes let me know he was speaking truth. I wanted to burst into laughter, but I held it in. He was so gullible. And whipped. This man fell for me hook, line, and sinker.

Smiling at him, I said, "You don't know how happy I am to hear that."

"I mean it."

"I know," I responded.

"I can prove it to you tonight by bringing you to the church revival with me."

Aden had never shown up to church with a female on his arm so for him to want to bring me said a lot. Not only would it let everyone know he was now taken, it would show his mother and Carson what we had was serious, even if I was playing a game with Aden's heart. If Carson didn't want me, then I would use his son to make him want me. Who knows, the rate we were going, I could end up being Mrs. Aden Reid.

"Will you come with me tonight?"

"What about your mother?" I asked, not really caring what she thought.

"What about her?"

"You know she can't stand me."

"My mother can't choose the woman I want to be with. I'm my own man. I told you this."

"You sure about that," I looked at him skeptically.

"I'm positive."

"Having your family against me is already issues in our relationship, Aden. I'm scared to take this thing further for you later on to drop me because that's what you family wants."

"I'm not going to allow my mother or anyone to stop me from being with the woman I love."

166

His eyes were gentle and gleaming back at me.

"I don't want my heart broken, Aden?"

Was I really saying this? I was starting to believe my own hype. But I couldn't lie, it felt good to have a man who genuinely wanted to be with me without any attachments hindering us from being together. Here I was playing games and maybe this wasn't a game that needed to be played if Aden was the man for me.

"I promise I won't hurt you. As of today, I'm your man and you are my woman. Now, will you come to church with me tonight Juliana?"

With a warm smile, I said, "I would love to."

Aden leaned in and kissed me with excitement. For the first time, I liked being in his arms. It felt right. It felt good and for a moment I didn't know what was happening. Could it be that a part of me was somehow falling for Aden?

Amelia

After putting away the grocery I bought after running several errands, I saw I had a couple of hours to get ready for the revival tonight. I wish I had time to cook some dinner before I left but tonight was going to be a sandwich night, unless Carson and I picked up something on our way home from church. Speaking of Carson, he should have been home by now. I wondered where he was.

Ascending the stairs to go to my bedroom, I passed by Dee Dee's room. Her door was open, which was unusually because she always kept it closed. I used to think she was trying to hide something us. Being noisy, I looked in. The bed was made, the curtains were pulled back and the room was neat. And it looked as though all of her belongings were gone. To make sure, I went deeper into the room and searched the drawers and walk in closet. Empty.

"Dee, Dee, are you here?"

Nothing.

"I got a present for you. Where are you?" I asked, knowing if she didn't come running after hearing I had something for her, then I knew she had to be gone. She didn't come running. She'd actually done it. That woman was finally out of my house.

A grinned crept across my face. Clapping my hands, I began praise dancing in the room.

"Hay Hay, thank you Lord. You have come through again for me," I said giving the Lord some praise. This long day immediately turned into a great one now that I knew she was gone. What a way to start the night?

Excited about this, I sauntered to my room and immediately began taking all my clothes off. It felt good not having to close the door, for fear someone was going to bust up in here. I stood in the middle of my bedroom stark naked. Freedom at last I thought, and it never felt so good. I never knew how much I missed walking around my house like this.

I went to my master bathroom to start my shower when I noticed something on my mirror. I walked over to the counter and saw it was a picture.

"What tha?" I said to myself.

I pulled the picture off the mirror to see who this was. Whoever he was, he looked just like my husband, almost identical. I flipped the picture over to see a name written on the back.

"Carson Reid?" I mumbled.

My heart immediately began to thump wildly in my chest.

"This can't be true," I whispered softly as I stared at the image trying to grasp what was going on.

"Babe, where are you?" I heard Carson call out to me.

His voice startled me, and I dropped the image in the sink.

Nervously picking it up, I manage to say, "I'm up here."

I scurried from the bathroom to the bedroom closet to grab a robe to wrap around myself. Before he could get in the room, I was sitting on the bed waiting for him to arrive.

"Today has been a day," he said when he entered. He immediately started undoing his tie. "I would love nothing more than to crawl in bed next to you and call it a night."

I watched him, seeing if there was something I missed with him. What was this article about and who thought it was in my best interest to read this.

Carson finally noticed my solemn demeanor and asked, "Amelia, are you okay, honey?"

"Dee Dee is gone."

"Really?" he asked in surprise. "So soon."

"Yep. Her room has been cleaned out, so I guess she's gone."

"I know you are happy."

"I was," I said timidly.

"Was? What's wrong?"

With a curious look, I asked, "Do you have something to tell me, Carson?"

"What are you talking about?" he asked, removing his cuff links from his collar shirt so he could take it off.

"If you are referring to my sister, babe, I'm sorry. I did give her more money than I originally told you I would, but she needed my help. I felt sorry for kicking her out, but I wanted to make you happy as well," he explained.

"I'm not talking about your sister. I'm talking about this," I said holding up the picture.

As soon as he saw it, he immediately turned two shades lighter.

"Do you know anything about that?" I asked coolly.

"Where did you get this?"

"Someone taped it to our bathroom mirror."

"Dee Dee," he muttered.

"So, she did this?" I asked.

He said nothing.

"Are you going to explain this to me?"

"Amelia, it's nothing," he answered, turning abruptly away from me with the picture still in hand.

"Have you forgotten how long we have been married?" I asked, noticing the muscles in his jaw clench. He did this when something bothered him or when something was really wrong.

"Honey, I know how long we've been married," he said tensely.

"Then you should know I can recognize when something shakes you. Why was that left for me to find?"

His back was to me. I couldn't see his face. But I could feel the mood in the room shift. The air was thick with tension.

"Talk to me, Carson," I said with a raised voice.

With hesitation, Carson said, "He is my bother."

"Your brother?"

"Yes."

"I thought you only had a sister, Carson."

"I do. My brother died many years ago."

"And you never told me about him?" I questioned.

"It was painful to talk about."

"But I'm your wife. You could have talked to me about it."

"You are right."

"How did he die?"

"He was killed," he admitted somberly.

"How? And why do the both of you have the same name?"

Turning to me, he said, "Amelia, look, can't we talk about this after church. We are already running late."

"Okay. We can talk about it when we get home, but you better have some answers for me."

"I promise I will," he said sincerely.

He rushed to the bathroom to take his shower, not bothering to continue to undress in the bedroom or walk in closet like he usually did. My husband was shook and all I could do was sit on the bed wondering what he hiding. As bad as I wanted this handled right now, I knew we had an obligation to our church. Again, another time church superseded what was going on in our household? When was I going to stop choosing the church first and put myself before our members?

Skye

I knew I may have been wrong by accepting the invitation to go to lunch with Dante. He called me after Ms. Wanda left. So did Seth. He went to our bedroom, packed an overnight bag and left without saying another word to me. So getting Dante's call was somewhat of a nice surprise in the midst of the storm brewing in my life. I didn't expect him to call so soon but the idea of lunch would be a nice change of pace for me.

I was telling myself this was two old friends getting together to catch up on old time. But in the back of my mind I was also wondering was I doing this to get back at Seth for what he did to me. It wasn't like I was going to try to sleep with Dante. I wasn't that type of woman. But what if I did. He was a very attractive man. I'd only had one partner in my life. Maybe I should do as my husband did and see if the grass was greener on the other side.

I busied myself with my cell phone and didn't notice Dante approach the table. It wasn't until he leaned down and planted a kiss on my cheek that I knew he'd arrived. I was taken aback by his greeting. More so because his lips felt good on me. That brief contact caused my body to tingle in places it shouldn't for another man other than my husband. Come to think about it, not even Seth made my body react the way

Dante just made me feel. I had to cross my legs beneath the table to control the sensation.

It wasn't until he sat across from me that I got a better visual of him. This man was so fine. His coffee complexion glowed, and his luminous smile brighten the room.

"Sorry I'm late."

"It's okay," I told him.

"No it's not. Here I ask you out to lunch and I'm late. It's not a good look if you ask me."

"Well, you made it and that's what counts," I smiled.

"You are looking lovely as ever," he complimented.

There was that feeling again, that tingle in places that shouldn't. Not for him. I shifted uneasily, hoping he didn't notice.

"Thank you. You look dapper yourself."

Dante was dressed in a pair a denim jeans, a white collar shirt and a black blazer. I loved his style, much different than Seth who wore suits every day. Nothing was wrong with that, but I liked a man who looked relaxed and not so serious all the time.

"So how's life been treating you?" he asked.

Instantly my mind went to my failing marriage.

"It's great," I lied. "What about you? How are things going for you? And how's your nephew doing?"

"I'm doing great. I'm happy to be here with you instead of at work. As for my nephew, he's much better."

"That's wonderful to hear," I said not knowing what else we could talk about. I was not good at this at all and wondered was this a good idea.

"Do you come here to eat often?" he asked.

"I do."

"Me too. I love there pastas. I think that's what I'm getting today."

"I haven't eaten their pasta before. I usually get a salad or the smoked salmon with vegetables."

"You're eating healthy, I see."

"I have to. I'm watching my figure," I said.

"Your body looks fine to me," he said in a way that made that feeling come back. The look he gave me was more than just a compliment. It was a hidden message in there somewhere and I was going to ignore it.

Picking up my menu, I began to scan it to take my mind off this good looking man.

"You seem nervous," he said as he looked seductively at me.

Was I reading too much into this situation or was he really trying to flirt with me I thought.

"Why do you say that?" I stammered. I looked around wondering where the waitress was. I wanted to order now but she was taking her sweet time coming to us. Remind me not to give her a nice tip.

"I can tell. You don't have to be nervous around me. We are old friends just catching up right?" he asked.

"Yes."

"I'm happy I finally get a chance to be next to you. I mean close to you," he stammered now.

A sly grin crept across his face and she dropped his head in embarrassment.

"What?"

"I don't know if I should say what's on my mind."

"Say it," I told him.

With his lips pressed together, he asked, "Did you know I had a major crush on you in high school?"

With my heart skipping beats, I said, "No, I didn't know that."

"I did. I wanted to ask you out so many times, but I thought you would tell me no because I wasn't the most handsome guy in school."

"You could have asked. I wasn't that type of girl."

177

"I didn't know that," Dante countered. "Too bad you are married now, or I would be asking you out to dinner too."

"Yes, too bad I'm married," I murmured, picking up my water and taking a sip.

The rest of our lunch pretty much went on the same way. We ate great food and I made sure to stick to my salad. When it was time to go, I wasn't ready for it to end but I knew it had to before I got myself in a situation.

Dante walked me to my car.

"Thank you again for having lunch with me."

"It was nice," I admitted.

"We have to do this again," he suggested.

"I don't know if that's a good idea," I said skeptically.

"Well, think about it. I'm a great cook. Maybe I can cook for you one evening."

"Okay," came out my mouth before I could stop myself. The surprise look on his face let me know he wasn't expecting me to say that either.

"So are we planning our next get together?" he asked cautiously.

Say no. Say no. Say no, I repeated in my mind, but my mouth betrayed me again.

"Yes, that's a plan," I said not sure why I was going along with this.

"My house?" he looked at me questioningly.

"Yes," I said again.

"Is tonight too soon? We might as well keep this reunion going," he said chuckling.

"Tonight sounds great."

And just like that, I was going to have dinner with a man that wasn't my husband. What was I doing? This was not the best thing to do if I was planning on getting my husband back into my life. Especially when I knew now he was probably with Fatima. Why should I care when he didn't? Dinner with Dante did sound great and for the first time in a long while, I was excited about something that brought me some happiness.

Amelia

The more I thought about, the more I wanted answers. I was not willing to wait until we got back from church revival. So when Carson entered out bedroom again, I demanded he explain what that picture was all about and how I wasn't willing to wait for him to explain himself. I could tell he didn't like it, but I didn't care.

By the time Carson explained everything to me, I was ready to pack my belongings and move back to North Carolina where I was originally from. I couldn't wrap my mind around what he was telling me. It was like I was married to a man I didn't even know. I'd truly been played. I fell for it hook, line and sinker. All because I loved this man and I trusted everything he'd ever told me was true.

The tears that streamed down my face weren't because I was sad. It was because I was enraged at the fraudulent relationship I'd had for the past twenty five years with this man. I married him. I loved him. I gave birth to his children. And now the man I knew to be Carson Reid wasn't Carson Reid at all.

"Baby, say something."

"What am I supposed to say, Carson? Whoever you are? That's not even your real name," I belted.

"But it is."

"No it isn't. You just sat here and told me your name was Benjamin Reid."

"I know I should have told you the truth from the beginning."

"You think?" I hissed.

"I was scared if I told you the truth, I would lose you."

"You didn't think I loved you enough to see pass your past, Carson?"

"I wasn't willing to take that chance. When I laid eyes on you, honey, I knew you were the woman I wanted to be with."

"It was the same for me. I would have walked whatever trenches with you, loving you even more for trusting in me enough to want to tell me what you'd done. But now…" I paused.

"Now what?" he questioned.

"Your years of lies may cost us our marriage," I threatened.

"Please. Don't say that," he said with his eyes begging me not to leave him.

"You were too busy trying not to lose me, only to lose me in the end," I told him.

"But it doesn't have to be like this. Everything is out in the open now and we can get past this."

"We. Don't you mean me? I'm the one who's been lied to all this time. My world has been turned upside down. How do you think that makes me feel?" I asked him.

"I don't know."

"Exactly. So for you to sit here and expect me to *get pass this*," I said putting my fingers up in quotations, "that's crazy to me."

"Look. I shouldn't have said it like that. As you can see, I haven't made the best decisions in my life. Where things turned around for me is when I met you and it's been a heavenly journey since," he stated lovingly.

"It was a journey paved with lies. You were selfish. You didn't give me the opportunity to choose if this was what I wanted. You thought that lie would remain dormant forever. You of all people know what's done in the dark will always come to the light. *For nothing is secret, that shall not be made manifest; neither anything hid, that shall not be known and come abroad.*"

"Luke 8:17," he murmured shamefully.

"Yes. You know this. So how did you think you would ever get away with this?"

"I got caught up, Amelia."

182

"That's what lying does, get you caught up to continue to lie once it's got you what you wanted. You've become so comfortable with things that it never crossed your man to disclose this to me."

"You are right. I can't argue with you on that. But honey, please don't leave me. You know I love you with everything in me. I know you love me too. Yes, I was selfish. I was wrong. I am whatever you say I am, but can you blame me for making the decision I made. I found you, the woman I wanted to spend the rest of my life with. I didn't want to risk losing you by revealing my shady past. I apologize for deceiving you. But I don't apologize for making the decision I did because I have the best life ever with the woman I love who gave me myself back. You have me love. You have me two beautiful children. You gave unconditionally, and I will not ever regret that."

"Unconditionally," I said to him. "Unconditionally means with limits. You put limits on us."

"I love you," he reiterated. Carson wrapped his arms around my shoulders as he sat next to me on the bed. "Amelia, I love you so much. Please don't leave me," he continued to plead.

"Is this what Dee Dee was talking about when she said she was going to get the last laugh?" I asked.

"Yes," he admitted.

"That's why you've always helped her like you have. She's known about you this entire time."

"Yes," he said again.

I shook my head in disbelief.

"So even knowing the threat she held over your head, at no point did you think I was worthy enough to know?"

"Amelia."

"You could have told me then, but you continued to live your lie. All this shows me is that you never intended on this getting out. That's why you were paying her off," I surmised." I began giggling to myself as I said, "I don't know if I can do this, Carson."

"Yes you can. Just because I'm not the person I've portrayed in name doesn't mean I'm not the person I am in the flesh," he replied. "What you see is what you have and that's a man of God who loves the woman God blessed him with. The only thing I've lied about is what I've told you."

I scanned his face and saw the genuine look on his.

"Let me continue to love you."

I didn't say anything.

"Please?" he begged.

A tear streamed down my cheek. Carson used his thumb to wipe it away before he kissed the place he touched. He then kissed my forehead and then my cheek again. Then his lips connected with mine. I didn't resist. As much as I wanted to, this was my husband, one I loved dearly.

"We can't do this," I feebly said.

"Let me love you," he whispered.

Carson gently laid me down on the bed. He kissed me over and over again. I return the passion and gripped the back of his head pulling him into me. He felt good. This felt good. My excitement quickly turned to nostalgia for Carson. His left hand gently made its way down to the core of my body and rested at the outer limits of my epicenter. I waited patiently for him to please me and it wasn't long before his fingers began to massage my region. My body arched with gratification as waves crashed throughout me.

Carson gawked at my reaction. I couldn't speak. I couldn't say anything because I was too wrapped up in enjoying the delight he was bringing to me. I knew falling for his advances was giving him the impression I was okay with what happened, but little did he know it wasn't. This was not the end of this conversation but for now, I would enjoy him and do what I did best as first lady by putting a smile on my face for my husband.

Amelia

Even though Carson and I made passionate love, the realization of what he revealed to me came flooding back on our way to church. Needless to say the car ride was a silent one because neither of us knew what to say. The only solace I got out of this ride was the soft gospel music surrounding us. God knew what I needed at this time as "I told the storm" began to croon through the speakers. This song hugged me like a warm blanket as the lyrics filled me with emotions. I closed my eyes and took in her words as I swayed back and forth resisting the urge to cry. I couldn't help but think about my marriage. What Carson revealed could affect not only our marriage but also our future within the church. I was in a storm right now and the rain was just beginning to fall. My spirit told me this the storm was just beginning but until then, I was going to pray and enjoy this song I knew God was playing on my behalf.

Carson's cell phone rung. This was the third time since we'd gotten into the car, but he sent each call to his voicemail.

"Why are you not answering phone?"

With everything I'd found out this evening, I was suspicious of everything. If he could lie about something as simple as his name, what else could this man be hiding.

"It's Dee Dee. I don't feel like talking to her right now. She probably calling to see how things went down with you and I."

"Do you want me to talk to her?" I asked.

"No. I'll talk to her later. I don't need her upsetting you with anything else."

"Is there anything else?"

White knuckling the steering wheel Carson cast a glance my way answering with a "No."

I looked at him skeptically. No, I looked at him because I knew there was something else he wasn't telling me. He wanted me to trust him, but I knew he was keeping something else from me.

I sat in my usually spot on the third pew in the center aisle of our church. A few members greeted me with small talk and some with hugs and kisses. I smiled weakly not feeling like dealing with anything tonight. What I didn't want to do was take my frustrations out of innocent people, so I prayed to the good Lord to please not let that happen.

The gospel music continued to lift my spirits but still wasn't enough to take away the saddened state I was in. To my dismay, sitting at the other end of this pew was Juliana. *Since when did she attend revival* I thought? I looked in the direction of who she was gazing at and saw my son Aden winking his eye at her. This unnerved me. Not only did I have to deal with the lies of my marriage, I had to deal with this harlot who'd sunk her fangs in my son. I closed my eyes and sent up more prayer because I didn't like being this upset in church. Not in God's house. It was bad enough to sin outside these walls but to have impure thoughts within this sanctum made me feel even worst.

When I opened them, I did feel a bit calmer. I knew the power of prayer. And I rebuked the devil steadily trying to pull the foundation from up under me.

"Lord I'm trying," I said to myself.

My mind raced from one issue to the next. I sat here realizing the position I held within this church was a lie. If this ever came out, people were going to think I was a part of this rues. I shook my head as a flurry of emotions bombarded me. Again, I resisted the urge to cry.

His brother I thought. Carson explained the picture was indeed his brother and that his real name was Benjamin Reid, not Carson. He took on his brother's identity because he was a felon. And by him being a felon, it was difficult for him to get a job or any other opportunity to get his life back on the right track. Door after door kept getting slammed in his face and it was then he realized why most felons ended up back in prison. No one wanted to give them a chance. He was one that learned from his mistake and needed that second chance to move on, but obstacles kept him down.

I'd heard stories like his before, mostly from my own family members who endured the same thing. Over half the men in my family were felons. Just because it looked like I was this elegant woman who carried herself with class didn't mean I forgot I came from the streets back in the day myself. I drank. I smoked weed. I even shoplifted in my day, but I was one of the lucky ones who never got caught doing my wrong. I could have been in his shoes, but I was spared, which is why it upset me that Carson couldn't confide in me about something like this. Hearing his story was much like my own. The only difference is I didn't have to pull any jail time behind my wrong doings.

Carson explained, "My brother died unexpectedly, which devastated me and Dee Dee. If it wasn't for our brother, we would have been homeless. He was helping us both out but when he died, it left is both in a tight bind. I didn't have a job because I couldn't get one with my record and Dee Dee was busy hustling men out of their money. The rent was coming up due and neither of us knew what we were going to do since he was taking care of us. It was then my sister came up with the idea for me to take on my deceased brother's identity. At first I thought this was crazy but when she began to explain all the hard times I was going through due to my record, I felt like I didn't have a choice. It wouldn't be too hard since he and I looked identical. There was no other family besides Dee Dee and I, so this would be our secret until death. Or so I thought."

I understood why my husband did it. What I didn't understand was why he continued to escalate the fraud if he got away with stealing his brother's identity. You see, not only did he take on his brother's name, he also falsified document proving he was an ordained minister. That's right. Carson was not a true pastor.

Granted, he knew the word and preached his behind off. He said he had nothing else better to do in jail but turn to the Lord and learn the bible from front to back. He had an amazing gift and was one of the best preachers around our city, if not the best preacher around. But his positioned was based off trumped-up information as well. The word he was preaching was truth, yet, he still perpetrated a lie because of who he portrayed himself to be. He was created by God, who claimed to be a man of God, who lied every time he perform as a pastor. I knew if this ever got out, regardless of how good he was, people wouldn't be able to look past the deception. I'd spent years with him and found it difficult to get pass it, so I knew the members of our congregation wouldn't let this slide.

Then another thing occurred to me. This also meant any formal things he'd done, say for instance a wedding, was not legal because he was not legitimate?

I asked him, "You were going to perform our daughter's wedding weren't you?"

"I wanted to, but I knew I couldn't," he admitted.

"You agreed to it."

"I tried to get out of it, but my baby girl wanted this."

"Would you have done it anyway to keep up your lie?" I asked.

Carson paused before saying, "I don't know. I've been thinking about that. I didn't want to hurt Payton but again, I never thought my lie would ever come out."

"So your answer is yes."

He said nothing.

"Job 4:8 says *Even as I have seen, they that plow iniquity, and sow wickedness, reap the same.*"

"Amelia," he called out, but I ignored him.

"Matthew 7:15 says *Beware of false prophets, which come to you in sheep's clothing, but inwardly they are ravening wolves.*"

Carson's head dropped.

"Did any of these scriptures cross your mind as you walked every day with your head held high knowing you were an impostor?"

"It did but…"

"Not only were you willing to hurt me, but you brought that drama into our children's lives. You were willing to perform the marriage of our daughter in order to keep your secret. Do you know the damage you would have done to her?"

A tear streamed down my face as I thought about our conversation earlier. I reached in my purse and pulled out a handkerchief to dab away my tears. Lucky for me, the choir was singing, and the tears people saw coming from me could be seen as me getting filled up with the spirit, not knowing I was filled up with overwhelming emotions.

I looked up at the podium and watch Carson do his thing as he looked back at the choir and clapped his hands to their inspirational melody. People were standing and shouting and giving praise as this revival was something to be thankful for. But I couldn't be thankful. Not after what I'd just found out.

I was jolted out of my thoughts when I felt a hand on my shoulder. I turned to my left to see Skye standing there.

"Can I sit down beside you?" she asked.

"You sure can," I said moving over to let her have my spot. From the somber expression on her face, Skye was not having a good day either. There was no doubt her drab demeanor had something to do with what was going on with her and Seth.

Another thought struck me. Skye's marriage was a fraud as well. Carson performed her wedding. How could I look in this young lady's face and pretend like I didn't know this about my husband? Wouldn't keeping this lie make me part of his deception too.

I could see how easy it was for Carson to keep this going. It was easier to live the lie he started rather than admit the truth and destroy many lives, one of them including Skye, who I cared for deeply. I had to make a decision. I had no choice but to stand by my husband, even if it meant acting like I didn't know the truth about him. I knew this may not have been right, but the ladder was more difficult to fathom. I just prayed I wasn't condemning my soul to hell for the decision I'd just made.

Skye

When the revival was over, I felt more refreshed than I had all day. It was nothing like getting filled up by the word to elevate your spirit. And I needed some uplifting. Especially after I watched my husband pack the rest of his belonging to move in with his mistress.

I couldn't help but think this was Fatima's plan all along? It was mighty convenient my marriage ended up being the fall guy here. Did she know the outcome was going to be Seth leaving me for her, the reason why she had me show up to her home and catch the two of them together?

"It's so good to see you, Skye. How are things with you?" First Lady Amelia asked tenderly.

"Things are okay," I nodded dubiously.

"Are you sure, honey, because your body language and that knit in your brow is telling me otherwise."

Smiling weakly, I said, "Seth moved out today and asked me for a divorce."

"He did what?" she asked in shock. "Are you kidding me?"

"I wish I was. He left me for this mistress," I told her.

"I am so sorry to hear this," she said genuinely.

"Please don't feel sorry for me because I'm good. He may have left me, but I haven't given up on our marriage. When I said my vows before God I made a promise to him and that means more to me than the fling my husband thinks he loves right now."

"I admire you, Skye. A lot of women would walk away but you are fighting for your marriage, which is one of the hardest things…" she said pausing. Her eyes began to fill with water.

"Mrs. Reid, are you okay?" I asked placing a comforting hand on her shoulder.

"I'm fine, honey," she said. "Just filled up with your words is all. Sometimes it's good to be reminded about some things, you know."

I nodded, wondering where this emotion was coming from. Mrs. Reid always seem to have it together but tonight she seemed somber. Here she was checking on me and I needed to ask her how she was. The ones who tended to take care of everyone else seldom had anyone to take care of them.

"Mrs. Reid, are you sure? I hope you don't mind me saying but your body language too is telling me you are not okay."

With a softened tone, she said, "I'm going through some things myself right now."

"I'm here for you. As much as you have been here for me, this is the least I can do."

Smiling weakly she said, "You have helped me more than you know."

After a few more words, Mrs. Reid and I parted ways. As hard as she was trying to put on a brave front, I knew something had her troubled. I understood her wanting to be private, since she was the first lady, so all I could do was pray for her and whatever she was going through.

On my way to my car, I heard someone call out to me. Feeling uneasy, since it was dark, I clicked the key to unlock my car and hurried to get in. Church parking lot or not, people were crazy everywhere. With one leg in my ride, the person called out to me again and this time I recognized the voice.

"Skye, wait."

I turned to see it was Dante. He was jogging over to me.

"Dante?" I questioned.

I stepped out of my car and closed the door waiting for him to approach.

"I thought that was you," he said.

"What are you doing here?" I asked noticing he was in some jogging pants and a tee.

"I'm here to pick up my mom."

"She goes to church here?" I asked.

"Nawh. She came with a friend of hers to attend the revival here. Do you go to church here?"

"Yes. This was why I had to cancel on our dinner tonight. I complete forgot about the revival. Did you get my message?"

"I did. I was devastated of course but look at God. He still managed for us to cross paths again."

"For a minute, I thought you were stalking me," I joked but was serious at the same time.

"Could you blame me? I mean, look at you. You are a beautiful woman," he complimented.

This man sure knew how to make a woman feel good. I knew I was blushing as I grinned ruefully.

"At least I could make you smile."

The way he was looking at me was making me nervous. A couple of church ladies walked by saying goodnight, all the while staring. I knew they were wondering who he was and why I was talking to him since I was a married woman. The last thing I needed were rumors going around the church I was stepping outside my marriage. Church was a place of worship but unfortunately, it was also a place of drama, started by noisy people like the two ladies that just walked by.

"Look, I need to be getting home," I told him.

"I know your husband is wondering where you are."

He was fishing and all I did was nod, knowing Seth didn't have me on his mind at all since he was with his mistress. The thought saddened me.

"Did I say something wrong?" he asked noticing my uncheerful disposition.

"I'm fine. Just tired."

"You sure I didn't say something wrong?" he asked.

Pausing, I debated whether to say something to him, but a woman called out to Dante. He turned while I looked over his shoulder to see an elderly woman waiting on the sidewalk for him.

"I'm coming Mama. Give me a sec," he said.

Dante turned back to me giving me his full attention.

"You were saying."

Smiling, I said, "It's nothing."

"You know you are on the church lawn right. You can't lie on God property," he joked.

"I'm not trying to unload my issues on you. Besides, your mother is waiting and I'm not trying to have her mad at me."

He looked back, and his mother had her hand on her hip gawking in our direction, a sure sign she was getting irritated.

"I guess you are right. I better get her home," he said. "But this conversation is not over."

"Okay."

"Are you coming to church tomorrow?" he asked.

"I want to but I'm not sure."

"Maybe I'll put on a suit and step foot up in here."

"Don't come for me. You need to come for yourself," I added.

His mother called out to him again, this time her voice filled with frustration.

"It kills me how people get inpatient when you are the one doing them a favor," he joked.

I chuckled.

"I better be going before she really embarrasses me out here and I'm not trying to look like no fool in front of all these church folks. It was good seeing you again, Skye."

"Good seeing you too," I responded.

"I'll talk to you soon."

"We will see," was all I can say.

Dante smiled before leaning in and kissing me on the cheek. There went those tingles again. Backing away from me slowing, he turned to jog over to his mother. She instant started fussing at him for keeping her waiting and I chuckled at their exchange thinking about what was God up to.

Amelia

I stood outside my husband's office at the church and waited for Deacon Dwight to leave so I could retrieve Carson and go home. All I wanted to do was get out of these clothes and shoes and crawl into my bed.

"Praise the Lord," I heard a voice say and turned to see it was my sister in law Dee Dee.

As usually she looked posh dressed in a black pants suit and a wide brimmed hat. I wondered if any of the money we gave her to get on her feet was spent getting this outfit. She smiled happily, but I didn't see anything to smile about in this moment.

"Wow, Amelia, I mean First Lady. You were supposed to greet me back with a Praise the Lord," she stated.

I couldn't open my mouth for fear whatever spewed from it would not be God like. All I could do was pray in my head for the good Lord to give me strength to deal with this devil.

"I haven't seen you this quiet in…in…you've never been this quiet. You always got something to say. Who's stolen your joy?"

"What do you want, Dee Dee?" I asked curtly.

"I'm just trying to have a conversation with my family."

"I see you are dressed in all black. I thought I felt an evil presence in my midst."

"I thought I was going to someone's funeral today, but I guess not," she shot back.

"Be careful about going to those funerals. You could be dressing for your own."

Dee Dee eyes narrowed.

"Is my brother in there?"

"No. I'm standing here because I have nothing else better to do," I said sarcastically.

"I need to talk to him. He owes me some money."

"Owes you?" I dropped my head knowing we'd paid her generously.

"That's what I said," she scoffed.

"After," I said louder than I intended to. I paused to regain control of my emotions. Lowering my tone, I continued. "After what you did to him, to us, you think he's going to hand you more money."

"Yes," he said flatly.

I stepped to her and smiled so if anybody came around the corner to see us, it would look like were having a pleasant conversation.

"Everything is out. I know the entire story about what you two did. How dare you use this against him for your own benefit? But, I guess I shouldn't expect anything less coming from a parasite like you."

Dee Dee kept the devious smirk on her face.

"How can you be sure you know everything?" she asserted.

What was that supposed to mean I thought? I did think he was holding something else back from me. Could she know what that was?

"Amelia, I've never liked you. I only tolerated you because you married my brother. Your marriage wouldn't exist if it wasn't for me. My brother is who he is because of me. If you think I can't bring your world down even more, you are dumber than I thought. Carson doesn't have to pay me but trust and believe I can destroy the both of you and would be happy to do so just to see the wounded look on your face. That alone would give me pleasure."

It took everything in me not to snatch her pompous behind up. A couple of staff members turned the corner and smiled at the two of us as they passed. I hoped they didn't see how irate I was at Dee Dee.

"That's a good little First Lady. Act like you have it together when we know that's so far from the truth. You are nothing but a fraud just like my brother."

The door to Carson's office opened and Deacon Dwight proceeded to exit. Both of them were chuckling about something but Carson's smile waned when he saw his sister and I together.

"You ladies have a goodnight," the deacon said.

"You do the same," I responded.

Dee Dee lustfully eyed the deacon who seemed to be taken by her as well. Dee Dee put her fingers up to her ear like she was holding a phone and mouthed for him to call her. He grin mischievously as he nodded.

"Please, come into my office."

I stormed pass my husband while Dee Dee sauntered into the space cockily. Carson closed the door behind us. I didn't waste any time speaking what was on my mind.

"Why are you still giving her money, Carson?"

"She needs our help."

"Haven't we helped her enough? She's lived rent free for months. You paid for her place to stay and didn't you give her five thousand dollars on top of that?" I asked heatedly.

His eyes darted back and forth between his sister and me.

With a perplexed expression he said, "Yes."

"So what did she spend it on? What is she doing, trying to live the lifestyles of the rich and famous?" I said glaring her way.

"Baby, please calm down," he coaxed.

I knew I was getting loud. Acting a fool up in the church was not something I did but the devil was testing me. Unfortunately he was winning because I was on the verge of exploding.

"Carson, please give me my money so I can go," his sister demanded. "I got some things to do and people to see."

"Who, Deacon Dwight?"

"As a matter a fact, yes."

"The man is married."

"That's not my problem. That's his wife's issue. Now Carson, where is my money?" she held her hand out.

My husband walked over to his desk. He reached in the drawer and pulled out a check. Passing it to Dee Dee, I snatched it out of his hand before her grubby little fingers could get a hold to it.

Looking at the amount, I was flabbergasted.

"Ten thousand dollars. You are giving her ten thousand dollars?" I belted.

Without hesitation, I ripped the check into pieces. Both Carson and Dee Dee's mouth fell open as I dropped the torn fragments to his desk.

"What are you doing?" Carson droned.

"I know you didn't rip my check up?" Dee Dee spat.

Ignoring his sister, I asked, "What else is she holding over your head, Carson?"

He didn't answer. He dropped his eyes to the floor and rubbed the back of his head.

"Tell me, Carson," I demanded.

"This is not the time or place to talk about this, Amelia. Have you forgotten where we are? We are in a church and we need to act like it."

"I'm not leaving until you write me another check," Dee Dee replied, lowering herself in one of the chairs.

"My check book is at home," Carson informed.

"The church doesn't have checks?" she asked.

"Dee Dee, I'm not going to use the churches money. I have my own. You can either leave here with nothing or follow me home to get your money."

She sighed standing to her feet.

"Okay. I will meet you at your house. You better not be playing with me, Carson. I want my money. And hurry up because I told you I have something to do," Dee Dee said sternly as she exited the space.

Carson stepped around his desk to approach me. He reached out to touch me, but I stepped out of his grasp.

"Honey, please."

"Don't please me. It's a reason why you keep giving her money and I want to know why?" I affirmed.

"Let me take you home and we can talk there."

We were interrupted by a knock at his door and turned to see Aden standing there with non-other than Juliana.

Juliana

"Mom? Dad? Is everything okay in here?" Aden asked his parents with concern. Both of them looked sullenly our way. His mother appeared upset while Carson looked like he'd lost his best friend.

Was there trouble in paradise? Could this be the beginning to an end with them two? Maybe I was giving in to Aden too quickly. Now that I could see something was foul between Carson and his wife, maybe I still had a chance with him. Could I be getting my wish after all? It appeared Carson was going to be mine a lot sooner than I thought.

"Son, everything is fine. We got some bad news a moment ago," Carson addressed.

Aden shifted his gaze to his mother for assurance. She smiled weakly at him but didn't say anything.

"You okay, mom?"

"I'm fine, sweetie. Don't worry about me. Tell us what are you doing here?" she asked changing the subject.

Aden gazed at the two of them as if he didn't believe them. He shouldn't because they were lying to him. I wished he'd push the issue more, but I knew he wouldn't.

"I wanted to talk to the two of you about something."

Amelia's gazed shifted to me and traveled the length of my body. She had to know this conversation had to do with me since I was here with her son.

"Come in son and closed the door," Carson commanded.

Walking around to take position at the head of his office, Amelia stood by Carson's side. He looked honorable in his leather chair, the same one I'd dreamed about pleasing him in many time. The two of them tried to appear united, I knew better. Carson seemed uneasy. That could have been because I was here. It could also be due to what Aden and I walked in on.

"Okay, son. What would you like to talk to your mother and I about?" Carson asked leaning back in his chair with his hands clasped together.

Aden turned to me, taking my hand into his. Smiling, he winked at me before addressing his parents.

"I wanted to let you know Juliana and I have decided got become exclusive."

Amelia drew in a breath of agitation. Carson on the other hand seemed unfazed.

"What do you mean, exclusive?" his mother asked giving me a contemptuous sneer.

"We are dating. She and I are a couple."

Both stared at us but neither said anything causing an uncomfortable aura to fill the room.

"I know you two, especially your mom, don't care for Juliana but she's the woman I want to spend my time with. I hope you can respect that," Aden added.

"Respect," his mother chuckled.

"Amelia," Carson warned.

"Respect is something that is lacking within this family lately."

"Don't do this, Amelia," Carson advise.

I smiled deviously as the friction between them spilled into the open for us to view. The foundation was cracking, and this thrilled me.

"How long have you known her?" Amelia prodded.

"What do you mean?" Aden asked.

"How long have you known her, two days, a week, a year, what?" she snapped.

"I've known her for a while as a member."

"And this has nothing to do with you trying to use your member with her? That is what she's known for, sleeping around."

"Mom," Aden called.

Carson called out to her as well, but Amelia ignored him.

"Don't forget where you are?" Carson reminded.

"I know exactly where I am. God knows my heart. He knows what's on my mind so if I'm thinking it, I might as well address it," she admitted.

"This is still our church."

"And Aden is our son. He was here long before this church came into the picture. This boy doesn't know what he wants."

"Yes I do," Aden said but Amelia ignored him.

"He's thinking with other parts of his body that's obviously draining the blood from his brain because he's lost his mind to get involved with her."

I'd had enough of her putting me down, giving me the cold shoulder and evil glares. I wanted so bad to tell her your husband and son in law must have lost their minds too because I'd slept with the both of them, but I maintained. Maybe it was Jesus keeping me from exposing the dirty truth of Carson who kept looking at me in fear that I would say something. Unlike the First

Lady, I was going to conduct myself in a more respectable manner.

"Amelia, tell me. What have I ever done to you?" I asked sweetly.

"You got your claws into my son," she shot back.

"You didn't like me before we became an item."

"Maybe that's because I know what you are all about."

"What's that?" I questioned.

"Ladies, please," Carson interrupted but Amelia kept going.

"You have a reputation that far surpasses any street walker in this city."

"Mom!" Aden bellowed.

Carson stood saying, "That's enough. We are not doing this here."

"You manning up now?" Amelia challenged him. "The time you should have been manning up was when your sister was here. But you want to step to me like this."

Carson recoiled like a child as Amelia grimaced at him. She looked as though she could rip him a new one as angry as she was. This was more than Aden and I dating. This was something more devastating in the midst.

"Are you okay with our son seeing this woman when we both know she's been with quite a few of the men in our congregation."

Including yours, I thought.

"Mom, I'm not going to allow you to talk about Juliana like this."

I stood saying, "It's okay Aden."

"No it's not," he disagreed. "My mother is dead wrong for this. Have you seen her with any man besides me?"

"I don't have to. I know women like her. You want a come up and you are using my son to do it."

"She's not using me," Aden corrected.

"Being the first lady and a woman of God, I would think you wouldn't be naive enough to go on hearsay Mrs. Reid."

Amelia stepped around the desk and attempted to approach me. Carson grabbed her arm to stop her, but she jerked away from him. Aden maneuvered in from of me shielding me from his mother's angry demeanor.

Acting like Aden wasn't between us, she muttered, "I don't need here say. My spirit tells me something is not right with you. It's not that I don't like you. I don't

213

want you anywhere near me or my family. You are evil. I can feel it," she snarled. "I might not be able to keep you out of this church, but I can try my best to keep you away from me and mine."

I frowned at this woman wanting so badly to knock her down off her religious high horse. She didn't realize she was the common denominator in the reason the men in your life were fleeing like captured victims.

I cut my eye at Carson. His eyes begged me to let this thing go. He knew what I was capable of. I could ruin them all with one statement. Eyes ablaze, I gave him a look he better get his wife in check before I ended up hurting everybody up in here with the devastation I could drop in them right now.

Carson took the hint and trudged over to Amelia.

"Honey, let's go home," he suggested.

"Get your hands off me," she jerked away again.

He backed up off of her. With look of contempt and loathing, Amelia breezed pass Aden and I storming out of the church office leaving the rest of us standing there speechless.

Skye

I didn't know what else to do or where to go. Yes, I had a home to go to, but it wasn't a home without my husband in it with me. Instead, he was with Fatima. I sat outside in front of her house, watching, waiting to see any sign of Seth. A shadowy image would suffice. I wanted him. I needed him and didn't understand why he was choosing her over me.

Turning the bottle to my lips, I gulped down the clear liquid and relished the burn as he slide down my throat. A couple of droplets fell from mouth and onto my white silk blouse. Now it wasn't perfect, just like our marriage.

"God, I don't understand. Why would you do this to me? Haven't I been faithful? Haven't I given my best and gave my all to everything in my life. Yet, I've had nothing but strife. My father left when I was a baby. My mother died six years ago, and I don't have any siblings I can call to talk to about my problems. I have no one. Yet, I've done everything for everybody only to be hurt again."

I turned the bottle up to my lips again, trying to gulp the alcohol down quickly. I could feel the effects of it and hoped it would numb my feelings of inadequacy.

"I can't let him do me like this. I just can't."

Fumbling to put the cap back on the bottle, I tossed the bottle in the passenger seat. I opened the door to get out and made my way to the door.

"Skye?" Fatima greeted, looking at me dumbfounded.

"Is Seth here?" I asked, trying to keep it together as the effects of the alcohol were making me feel loopy.

"Yes, he's here," she said cautiously looking at me. Then she noticed what I was holding.

"Can I see him please?"

She stepped back and let me come into her place.

"Who is it baby?" Seth asked.

He had the nerve to look like he was right at home, wearing the basketball shorts I'd purchased him and a black tank. He stopped dead in his tracks when he saw it was me.

Sighing in frustration and said, "Do I need to get a restraining order against you, Skye?"

Ignoring him, I traipsed over to him and attempted to plant my lips on his. He leaned back pushing me away from him.

"Have you been drinking," he asked.

"Just a little bit," I whispered with a smile.

"You don't drink."

Null and Void

"I do now," I informed him.

"Skye, you need to leave."

"Baby, come on. You know you missed me. I can show you how much I missed you."

Seth peered around to Fatima who was standing back ogling us.

"Show me where you sleeping, baby," I told him.

"Why?" he asked.

"Because I'm here to spend the night with you."

"Uhm, Seth. What is going on? Did you invite her over here?" Fatima asked looking displeased.

"No, I didn't."

"Which one of you is going to show me where Seth sleeps?" I asked.

"I don't know what's going on here, Seth, but you need to handle her, and I mean now," Fatima griped as she trekked pass the two of us leaving us alone.

"See you, Fatima girl," I said waving.

Seth snatched me by the arm jerking me really hard.

"You're hurting me," I told him feeling pain radiated through my bicep.

"What do you think you are doing?"

"I'm trying to be with my husband."

"I told you we are over."

"I didn't agree to this. When I married you, Seth, it was till death do us part. I love you, honey. We need to work on making our marriage work," I explained.

"Don't you get it? Marrying you was a mistake," he admitted.

His words cut deep but I ignored this pain. The alcohol assisted in numbing his hurtful banter.

"I married you because I thought it was the right thing to do."

"You made love to me. You had to love me when you said those vows to me."

"I got what I wanted, which wasn't worth my time, Skye. I've found someone who is."

"You left me because I wasn't enticing enough?"

"Skye, it's that and more. Look, I'm tired of talking to you about this. It's obvious you are not getting it. Especially now that you have been drinking. This is not you."

"But it is. You created his," I gestured towards myself. "You made me drink."

"I didn't put the bottle up to your mouth. You did that."

"It's because I miss. Please come back home to me."

"You will get pass this."

"You haven't given me the opportunity to fix this."

"I've moved on and I think you should too. The divorce papers have been filed. You should be receiving them any day now."

I looked at him in disbelief.

"Please understand, I love Fatima. Maybe you can find a guy who will love you like you supposed to be loved but that guy is not me."

I pushed him in his chest yelling, "Why her and not me?"

"She's different."

"She's fat," I blurted. "Look at me. I'm a dime piece. And you go for her."

"You see. This is why I refuse to talk to you. You are not going to disrespect her in her own house," he said grabbing my arm again. He tried to pull me towards the door, but I struggled against his grip.

"I'm not leaving," I told him trying to jerk my arm loose, but he was too strong. "Let me go, Seth. You are hurting me."

He mange to get me to the door. He opened it and attempted to shove me out the door.

"Let me go," I yelled again, this time reaching around and smacking him in his face.

He reacted with a back hand across my face. The impact from his blow caused me to crash into the doorway before tumbling to the porch in pain. I held my cheek looking up at him, not believing he had the audacity to put his hands on me.

Stuttering with wide eyes, Seth said, "Skye, I'm sorry. I didn't mean to do that."

"You hit me?"

"I swear, I didn't mean to. I reacted. Baby, I'm sorry," he apologized again but I didn't want to hear it. If this was how he wanted to play me, then game on.

Null and Void

Juliana

Aden was not happy about how things went down
with his parents, especially his mother. Neither was I.
The nerve of her thinking she could come for me. She
was lucky I cared for Carson enough to keep my mouth
shut. I don't know why I did him this favor since he was
avoiding me. I'd called Carson several times and he
wasn't accepting any of my calls. He was sending me to
voicemail where I left messages for him to call me to talk
about us. I knew he was surprised to see me at the
revival since I was an only attend church on Sunday kind
of woman. He didn't know I was there with Aden.

The more I thought about not disclosing our
relationship to Amelia, the more I regretted not blowing
our little secret out of the water. It would have given me
joy to see the devastated look on her face. Now knowing
there was tension in paradise for their marriage, it was
time to make moves to get what I wanted.

It was no better way to make Aden feel better than
to give him what he wanted and that was me. I was eager
to please him in any way he wanted. Aden kicked off his
shoes and ripped at his blue button down shirt as we
kissed passionately in my bedroom. His excitement was
evident as he pants tented towards me. I smiled
flirtatiously waiting for him to mount me.

"You don't know how much I've wanted you," he confided.

"Then take me, baby," I urged.

Like an obedient pet, Aden sandwiched his body with mine. He kissed me fervently. He was definitely taking his aggression out on me, but it worked in his favor. He was showing me he could possibly satisfy me.

"Ouch," I heard him say and wondered what his outburst was about.

"What's wrong?" I asked.

"Something stuck me," he said standing to his feet.

I climbed off the bed to stand with him and watched as he pulled the covers back to see what stuck him. What he found was the undoing of our night.

Aden picked up the object from my sheets and examined it. His expression went from one of confusion to one of rage.

"Why is this in your bed?" he asked darkly with his brows furrowed.

"What is it?"

"It's a cuff link"

"I don't know how it got there," I stammered anxiously.

Aden closed the gap between us, jetting towards me. He grabbed me by the throat and didn't stop moving until my body slammed into the wall.

"Aden, what are you doing?"

"Where did you get this cuff link from?" he snarled.

"I don't know."

"This is my father's," he bellowed. "Are you sleeping with him?" he asked angrily.

"No. What are you talking about?" I asked breathlessly.

"This belongs to my dad."

"It could be someone else's," I tried to reason. His grip tightened around my throat.

"This was special made. I gave it to him two Christmas's ago. It has his initial on it. They are one of kind. There are no duplicates, which could only mean one thing. This cuff link is his," he emitted.

The treacherous expression he had on his face scared me. My heart drummed in my chest. I'd never seen Aden, nor any other man look this mad.

"Aden, please," I begged.

"Do I have to choke the truth out of you or are you going to tell me if you are sleeping with my father?"

I said nothing, fearing the repercussion of my answer. I didn't think things were going to turn out like this. Yes, I planted Carson's cuff link in my bed hoping Aden would find it and go running to tell his mother, but I didn't expect him to become violent with me. I didn't see this side in Aden. All I expected was for him to be devastated and tell his mother, so she would leave Carson. Boy, was I wrong.

Squeezing tighter, cutting off my air completely, I struggled to breath.

"If you think I won't choke the life out of you, you are sadly mistaken. I can kill you and get away with it. Trust me because you will be considered just another dead hooker with your reputation."

His words offended me. I may have been promiscuous, but I wasn't a hooker.

I clawed at his hands, but Aden's rage overpowered any hope of me thinking I could get out of this without admitting the truth.

"Okay," I mouthed.

"You going to talk now?" he asked.

I nodded feverishly. He loosed his grip and I struggled to suck in a breath of air. Tears streamed down the sides of my face as I panted eagerly. Aden didn't let me go completely, only enough to give the answer he'd been waiting on.

"Are you sleeping with my father?" he asked languidly.

Nodding fearfully, I whispered "Yes. Yes, I'm sleeping with your father."

Amelia

I sat in the passenger seat of his car in front of our home processing, yet another secret Carson revealed to me. If there was ever a moment I felt like giving up on everything, that time was now. Dee Dee was waiting in our driveway when we arrived. She looking back to see when we were going to exit the vehicle. I noticed she got that car she wanted. No doubt on the money we'd given her, and this disgusted me.

I had no more tears to shed. All I felt was discouragement, devastation, and anger. My body and mind were defeated, and I didn't have the energy to deal with anything else.

"Amelia, say something," Carson said cautiously.

A moment went by with nothing said. He gaped at me with trepidation in his eyes. I knew he was wondering what I was thinking but even I didn't know. Everything was muddled. It was difficult to put things in order to know what to say. Then it came to me.

"Should I get tested?" I asked apprehensively.

"No. But you can if it will make you feel better. I've gotten tested every year and I promise you baby, I'm clean."

"Your promises mean nothing, Carson," I turned to face him. Our eyes locked, both sad and dismal.

"Baby, I'm sorry."

"I know," I said apathetically.

"What was I supposed to say? By the way, when I was in jail, I was intimate with a man."

Hearing him say that caused me to whence.

"Now you see why I didn't want to tell you."

"Are you gay?"

"No."

"How do you know?"

"Because I know. I love women."

"Women," I chuckled.

"You, Amelia. I love you and only you."

"You have ruined my life," I said softly.

"Baby, this doesn't have to ruin our lives. Look at what we've built," he said pointing to our home. "Think about the two beautiful children we created together, the years of love we had for one another, our church. Honey, can't you see we were made for each other."

I thought we were, until now. I thought my life was built on a solid foundation where the underpinning was a structure built by God. But God wouldn't do this. Our relationship was built on cheap material which was causing us to fall apart now. Some structures could be mended but some couldn't be repaired. At this moment I couldn't see us getting pass this.

"It all makes sense now, you taking in Dee Dee and doing whatever she wanted you to do."

"Amelia," Carson whispered.

"I'm not sure if I can continue with this marriage," I said getting out of the car.

Carson bolted out also, running around to my side to meet me. As I closed the door, his sister proceeded to exit her vehicle as well.

"It's about time. Do you think I have all night?" Dee Dee chastise. "Go in the house and give me my check."

"It's over Dee Dee. I'm not giving you any more money," Carson told her.

"Excuse me," she said in astonishment.

"I'm done. You are on your own now."

"I don't think you want to do that," she chuckled cockily.

"I'm tired of you using what's happened in my past against me. Everything is out in the open. And I mean everything," Carson admitted.

Dee Dee eyed me incredulously. All she got was anger from me. I knew she was no good, using her own brother's secrets to live the life she wanted. She was as trifling as I thought she was.

Attempting to call his bluff, she said, "I don't believe you."

"I don't care what you believe. I'm done," Carson said placing a comforting hand on the small of my back to lead me into our home. I didn't have the strength to push him away.

"So you wife knows you slept with a man," she said with evil intentions like she thought Carson was lying.

Both Carson and I paused and turned to face her. She was smirking until she noticed my expression didn't change. I wasn't yelling and screaming at Carson like this was another big revelation he didn't tell me about. I didn't give her no reaction. Her smiled vanished and I knew then she had nothing else to use to get her way.

"I've done nothing but be good to you and you do me like this," Carson spat.

Dee Dee's lips didn't part.

"I've taken care of you for as long as I can remember. You claim to love me but how you've treated me over the years is not love at all. It's greed," Carson said. "You've used my secrets for your own lucrative lifestyle and I'm done."

"Don't stand here and act self-righteous, bro. You are the one who lied this entire time."

"And you helped me carry on the lie, so I could take care of you."

Dee Dee shifted uneasy and leaned against her car crossing her arms to try to get a grip on what was happening.

"It's over Dee Dee. I'm done financing your life. If you don't know how to be a sister to me, then you will be nothing to me," Carson thundered.

I was surprised he stood up for himself. Even though it may be at the cost of our marriage, he had to be happy there were no more secrets hovering over him that she could use against him.

"I'll tell the church," she threatened.

Both Carson and I didn't say anything.

"I will go the local news and let everyone know what kind of liar you are," she roared.

He responded by saying, "Go ahead, Dee Dee. Do whatever you want to do. I don't care anymore. The one thing you will never do again is force me to do anything. What you fail to realize is if I lose my wife and kids, I've lost everything anyway. They are the most important things to me. Not the church, not my congregation, not the money and not you."

"Don't test me Carson."

He turned away from her.

"How am I supposed to make it? How am I supposed to pay my rent and pay for this car?" she asked frantically.

Ignoring her, he said, "Come on baby. Let's go in the house."

"You can't do this to me, Carson. I'm your sister," she screamed.

"Not anymore," and Carson shut do door leaving Dee Dee standing in the driveway penniless.

Skye

Yes, I called the cops on Seth. He never should have put his hands on me. I sat outside Fatima's house, and was still holding my face when the cops got there. His side piece tried to talk me out of it, asking me to come in her home and talk about it. She even offered me up some ice wrapped in a towel to apply to my swollen cheek. Seth didn't want to talk to me earlier, but he was all talk now. He apologized and said we could resolve this. Just like him, I was going outside of our marriage to have someone else resolved this issue. He went to Fatima. In my case I went to the police.

When I saw the officers walk Seth out of Fatima's house in handcuffs, I didn't feel any regret. I reveled in his misery. He broke my heart and now I was going to make him feel my wrath.

"She hit me," I heard him bellow. "I live here. She's the one who is trespassing."

His pleas fell on death ears as the officer loaded him in the back of the squad car.

"Are you sure you want to press charges, Mrs. Holden," the blonde police officer asked.

"Yes, I'm sure," I said angrily, wondering why he was asking me this again. I'd already told him I wanted to press charges. Usually the cops never hesitated putting a black man in jail but this time, they wanted to make sure this was something I wanted to do.

"You don't have to do this, Skye," Fatima belted from her front porch.

"Did you not see him hit me?"

"No," she responded.

"Of course you didn't. I should have known you would take up for him."

"If I saw him hit you, I would say so. Why would I want to get with a man who puts his hands on a woman?"

"I don't know. Maybe it could be for the same reason you slept with a married man in the first place," I retorted.

Fatima couldn't say anything. I turned my attention back to the officer in front of me who was looking back and forth between the two of us.

"And you said you are his wife?" he asked in a confused tone.

"Yes I am. She is his mistress," I said pointing at Fatima.

"Mrs. Holden, I think you should go and have your face examined."

"I'm good. I'm a doctor anyway so I know what I need to do," I said standing to my feet. "Is there anything else you need from me?" I asked the officer.

"No. I think we have everything we need."

"You need to test her. She's been the one drinking," Fatima disclosed.

That seem to catch the officer's attention.

"Ma'am, have you been drinking tonight?"

I wanted to lie and say know but knew they could give me a Breathalyzer to check. I was surprised he didn't smell it on me.

"Yes," I answered truthfully. "I never drink. I've been upset because my husband left me for her."

"Did you drive over here drinking?"

"No. I purchased the bottle and parked my car in front of her house and I started drinking here. I never drove under the influence," I explained, hoping he would believe me because it was the truth.

"Ma'am, I could arrest you. But because we don't have proof you were driving while under the influence, I'm going to let you go. Of course you know you can't drive yourself home tonight."

Nodding, I said, "I know."

"Can you call someone to come and pick you up?"

Camille instant entered my mind and I told the officer yes as I reached into my purse and pulled out my cell phone. To my dismay, I got her voicemail. I tried her number several more times getting the same result.

What am I going to do, I thought?

Then Dante came to mind. *I shouldn't call*, I thought. But what else was I going to do. Hesitantly, I dialed his number and he picked up on the first ring.

"Hello."

I didn't say anything.

"Hello," he greeted again.

"Dante," I murmured.

"Skye," he asked questioningly.

"Yes, it's me."

"Are you okay?" he asked with concern dripping from his voice.

"Not really. I need a ride. Do you think you can do me a favor and come pick me up?"

Without hesitation, Dante agreed. I gave him the address and sat waiting for him to arrive. I told the officer this and they all proceeded to leave the premise.

"Are you satisfied now?" Fatima asked.

"Yes. As a matter of fact I am," I said happily.

She shook her head with a smirk on her face and said, "You think this is a great way to get your husband back? No wonder you lost him," she said turning to walk in her house.

I quickly scurried in her direction yelling, "You took him from me."

"No. You gave him away."

"Come again," I said frowning.

"Your marriage failed because you are delusional. You have this picture perfect image of what you think it should be, but marriage is hard. There is nothing perfect about it."

"I never said it was. Besides, you don't know what I've done as a wife," I spat.

"I know you are not satisfying him in the bedroom. Seth described you as a cold fish. You just laid there and let him do all the work."

He told her that?

"I know you always have to plan things instead of being spontaneous. Tonight is the first time you've stepped out of your comfort zone. You drinking and coming over here has probably been the most spontaneous thing you've ever done. I'm impressed, and I think Seth is too even though you had him arrested."

"You will not try to tell me how I should be with my husband."

"So to be ex," she countered.

"I can't get blamed for the ill-fated actions of my Seth."

"That's true but you can't run the man away and wonder why."

"He didn't communicate how he felt to me. You of all people should understand that since your own husband did the same thing to you."

Fatima shifted uneasily.

"I guess I hit a nerve. What you need to admit is it doesn't matter what you do as a woman, wife, mistress, whoever. If a man wants to step out and leave the person they are with, they are going to do it. You can be the biggest freak, the most beautiful woman, the most affectionate mate ever and still lose your man for one reason or another. So please, spare me the lecture on what I could have done as his wife. Why don't you try to figure out why you switched roles from wife to mistress?"

A car horn blew, and I turned to see Dante in a black charger. Fatima's brows rose, which I didn't care. I knew she would take this bit of information back to Seth. That's exactly what I wanted her to do. He wanted me to move on. Maybe I would start tonight and see what Dante had to offer.

Amelia

There was no way I could stay in this house with Carson tonight. I stormed to my walk-in closet and jerked my suitcase from the top shelf. Positioning it on the floor, I opened it and began stuffing articles of clothing into it. I needed to get out of here. Getting as many things as I could fit, I pulled down a carryall bag also and took both pieces into the bedroom area where Carson was waiting.

"Please, Amelia, don't do this."

I said nothing,

"We can work through this, honey. Just don't leave me."

I rushed into the master bathroom and grabbed as many as my person hygiene items as possible. With my arms full, I brought it over to my carry bag and dropped the items into it. Going over to my dresser, I pulled out undergarments and stuffed that into the bag as well. Once done, I grabbed my bags, and brushed pass Carson like he wasn't in the room.

He tried to stop me when I carried my suitcase down the stairs to leave.

"Please, Amelia. You don't have to leave. I will leave."

It was a nice time to say this, after he'd watched me pack everything. Just like him to do things at the wrong time.

"I need to get out of this house and away from you," I said, tone flat.

"We need to talk about this."

"You had twenty five years to talk to me, but you didn't. Now, you want me to stay so you can explain everything. It's out now, Carson. I know everything, unless there is something else you need to disclose to me."

Carson eyes shifted from mine as we stood midway the steps with him blocking my way.

"What I need is for you to give me my space," I demanded, voice trembling violently. I pushed him, almost causing him to fall backwards on the stairs. For a moment, I was worried about him but once I saw he caught his balance, I wanted to kick myself for caring. I loved this man and it pained me that he could hurt me this way.

Carson bolted down the stairs and jumped in front of me again stopping me.

"Move, Carson," I yelled.

"Honey, where are you going?" he asked sincerely.

"I don't know."

"You don't have to do this."

"Yes I do. Now please, move."

I looked into his eyes, tears brimming wishing for once he would listen to me. With much regret, Carson pressed his lips together before stepping to the side to allow me to leave. When I began to walk pass him, he grabbed my suitcase causing me to look at him.

"I'll carry this for you."

Solemnly the two of us trudged to my car. I got in and opened the trunk, so he could place my luggage inside. Once the trunk was closed, Carson stood at the back of my car. He leaned against it, with both palms pressed on my vehicle, head down looking more depressed than I'd ever seen him before. I started my car, hoping this let him know I was ready to go. Looking back in my rear view, he looked up. Our eyes connected briefly. His pleaded with me to stay and mine told him I couldn't do this with him right now.

Clenching his jaw, he stood upright and stepped to the side. I backed away not looking at him once as I drove away. I didn't know where I was going. I thought about going to my daughter Payton's apartment but knew as soon as she saw me she would know something was wrong. There wasn't an explanation I couldn't give her at this time. The same went for Aden, who was probably with Juliana. I thought about my brother Diego and best friend Elaine but that would be the first place Carson would know to look for me. And I wasn't trying to cause friction between him and my brother. So I decided to get me a room at a hotel for the night. I think I might make that two nights. It was already late, and I knew I wouldn't feel like dealing with Carson tomorrow either. This way it would give me more time to think about how to move forward with our marriage.

The hotel room was very nice. A fluffy white comforter covered the king size bed as a flat screen TV was mounted on the wall. Tossing my bags to the bed, I immediately undressed so I could take me a hot shower.

I don't know how long I was in there. All I knew was I sobbed uncontrollable, getting the pain out of everything that transpired within the last few hours. I wished I could turn back the hands of time to go back to when things were good. Maybe the not knowing would have been better, then I wouldn't have to deal with this torment of thinking the past twenty five years of my life was a lie.

After my shower I crawled into the bed and turned on the television. Immediately Joyce Meyer appeared on the screen and I smiled weakly.

"What are you doing God?" I whispered softly.

I heard the buzz of my phone which was on vibrate. I picked it up off the bed and saw it was Carson calling. I hit ignore and placed my phone back down.

That was the eighth time he'd called me. He was not getting the hint I didn't feel like talking to him.

Another buzz of my cell came, and I picked up expecting it to be him again but saw it was my son Aden calling me this time. No doubt, Carson was using my son to find out where I was, and I wasn't falling for it. Not tonight. I would call Aden in the morning. I turned my phone off, not wanting to be bothered for the rest of the night.

Reclining on the bed, I closed my eyes to say a prayer. I didn't feel like praying. I knew that was sad, but I didn't. A part of me was upset with the way my life was playing out. I knew I wasn't a perfect Christian, but I was trying my hardest. This felt like even in my trying, I was still smacked in the face with issues that were ripping my world apart.

At the same time God was all I had. I had to go to him on everything that was happening because he was the only one who could guide me through this storm. I gathered my strength and swallowed my pride. I knew regardless of the struggled, God wouldn't leave nor forsake me. Nothing was too hard for him. And for the first time in hours, I smiled. Those were the exact words my brother told me in my dream the other night. Was this the reason for my dream? God saw this on my horizon and was preparing me. I let the joy of Jesus sweep over me and I prayed. No sooner than I said Amen, I felt a slight heaviness lifted from me. I was going to relish the moment. Thanking God for the brief moment of stillness, I drifted off to a peaceful sleep.

Juliana

I never dressed so fast in my life. I was putting on my clothes and calling out to Aden to stop him from leaving. I knew he was going to his parent's home, but I didn't want things to go down like this. When I got to my living room, my door was wide open. Aden had stormed out. I ran to the door and saw his car backing out of the complex. I screamed for him again, but he ignored my cries as he tires squealed away into the darkness.

I ran back in my home frantically searching from my purse which had my keys and cell phone. I didn't remember where I left it. Running back into my bedroom, I saw my purse on the floor near the edge of my bed almost complete under it. Snatching it from the floor, I ran as fast as I could to get to my car.

Back out, I desperately dialed Carson's number. It went straight to voicemail.

"Carson, answer your phone," I screamed.

I dialed his number again getting the same response. I kept hanging up and dialing him over and over again, but it was no use. Carson was not going to answer. So I decided to leave a message. I had to warn him about Aden.

"Carson. It's me. Look, Aden is on his way to your house. He knows, Carson. He knows," I shrieked into the phone.

Hands shaking, I hung up. Swallowing hard, I felt my throat was sore from Aden almost choking me to death. I pushed my car as fast as I could go, emergency blinkers on so I wouldn't get pulled by the cops. When I arrived at Carson's home, I saw Aden's car in the driveway. His car was still running, and the door was wide open. The music was blaring and when I looked up to the door of the home, I saw the front door was ajar.

I jumped out of my car and ran to the house. I heard yelling, like somebody was arguing as I made my way to the house. Then I heard what sounded like glass breaking. Entering the home, I ran to where I heard the commotion, which was upstairs. I took them two at a time and seconds later I was standing in a bedroom, which appeared to be the master.

To my dismay, Aden and Carson were locked like two pit bulls in a fight.

"Stop it," I screamed, scared to approach as punches were being thrown.

Aden scooped Carson and slammed him to the carpeted floor. Carson yelped in pain but didn't stop trying to whoop Aden's behind.

"Please stop," I yelled again but neither of them listened.

Aden stood and began kicking his dad in the side. He did this several times before Carson grabbed his foot. He twisted it, causing Aden to fall to the floor himself. This gave Carson just enough time to get the upper hand and pounce on top of Aden. Aden swung, hitting his dad in the face. Carson's reaction was to punch him back. The punch coming from Carson had a lot more power behind it and stunned Aden into submission. Carson punched him again and again. Aden was no longer fighting him back. I wondered was he passed out. I ran to Carson, jumping on him to stop him.

"You want to fight me?" Carson bellowed, with blood spewing from his mouth. "I will hurt you, son."

"Carson, please. Leave him alone," I pleaded, tugging on his arm to get him off Aden. "He's not fighting you anymore."

Carson stopped his assault, breathing hard as he struggled to his feet. Aden laid on the floor bleeding from his nose and moaning from the pain he felt.

"Get up since you man enough to put your hands on me," Carson demanded breathing heavily as anger outweighed love in this moment.

"That's your son, Carson. Don't hurt him."

Aden started to laugh. He held his stomach and rolled to his side and actually burst into laughter. Carson and I looked at him like he was crazy.

"I can't believe you dad," Aden protested. "I can't believe you would do mom like this. I can't believe you would do me like this."

"What?" Carson asked in confusion. "You came to my home, in my room, and swung on me without saying a word."

That was my opportunity to chime in.

"Carson, he knows," I informed him.

"Knows what?"

"He knows about us."

Carson's rage transformed into anguish.

"How? When? I don't understand," he stammered, stumbling back looking a rumpled mess.

"She told me dad. Juliana told me everything," Aden admitted.

His chuckles were now turning into cries of anguish.

"How could you cheat on mom?" he cried.

"Why would you tell him?" Carson said snatching me up by the arm.

"He made me tell him. He choked me. I didn't have a choice," I said now crying myself.

Teetering to his feet, Aden asked, "Where's mom?"

That's when it hit me she wasn't anywhere around.

"Your mother is not here," Carson replied glumly.

"It's late. Mom is never out this time of night. Why isn't she here?"

Carson said nothing, but his expression revealed he knew why she wasn't here.

"What did you do?" Aden fired off questions to Carson.

"Son, we can talk about this another time. What's going on between your mother and I is none of your concern."

"I swear, Dad, if you hurt her, I will kill you."

Carson stiffened at his son's words as a grimace crept across his face.

"Boy, don't you ever threaten me."

"Or what," Aden retaliated.

Carson walked towards his son. I jumped in front of him.

"Both of you need to calm down."

"And you need to get out of my house," Carson demanded.

"That's okay. Your little slut can stay. I'll leave. I need some fresh air anyway," Aden scoffed as he stormed out of the space leaving Carson and I alone.

Juliana

I walked over to Carson who was madder than I'd ever seen him before. He kept looking at the doorway to his bedroom where Aden stormed out of moments ago after threatening him. He dabbed at his busted lip, looking like he couldn't believe what just happened.

"Babe, let me see your lip," I said tenderly.

I reached up to caress his face, but Carson smacked my hand away backing away from me with a deep frown.

"What's wrong?" I asked in confusion.

"You are what's wrong. I knew I should have never got involved with you," he spat.

"All of this is not my fault, Carson."

"Whose fault is it then?"

"He found your cuff link in my bed," I told him. "He went into a rampage, choking me and everything. There was no way I could talk my way out of explaining why it was there. I can't help it if you carelessly left it there."

Chuckling deviously, Carson said, "There is only one set of cuff links I wear and those are the ones my son gave me. I remember putting them on a couple of days ago, Juliana. I haven't slept with you in months. So, please explain to me how my cuff link got into your bed when I know I didn't leave it there."

"I don't know. You were at my house, remember, when Rowan came over. You hid in my room. Maybe you lost it then."

"What did you do?"

"Why does that matter? Aren't you happy everything is out in the open?" I asked happily.

"How can I be happy about this, Juliana? My son and I got into fight over this. He thinks I'm the worst father ever."

"He'll get over it. Once he sees you are in love with me, he will eventually come around. Everything is going to be okay," I reassured.

"The only way things are going to be okay is if I get my family back."

"But…" I stuttered.

"I can't be with you knowing you've been with my son. Besides, I love my wife. I always have, and I always will."

With a nervous giggle I said, "You are upset right now and not thinking clearly. Why don't you let me help you forget about everything that happened tonight," I approached him again?

It was something about being in his home, in his bedroom that turned me own. I could see myself living here, lying next to him and being the next Mrs. Reid. He didn't need his wife or his kids. He could start fresh with me. I would give him all the kids he wanted. He needed to understand I could make him happy enough to forget about all of them.

Carson allowed me to approach him. My body pressed against his. I felt every muscle in his body tense but the one I hoped grew didn't.

"Relax, babe," I told him.

He fixed his eye on me, just like he did when we made love for the first time and this made me happy. I leaned forward and kissed his chest. I could feel the rapid beat of his heart and the sensual sigh he released when my lips connected to him. He didn't resist, letting me know he was enjoying this. But when I leaned in again to plant another kiss on his chest, he pushed me away. He had a look of loathing. I didn't understand why he was looking at me in this way.

"Carson, honey. What's wrong?" I asked.

Menacingly he said, "Do you think I'm going to fall for your games?"

"I'm not playing..."

"I know you planted my cuff link in her bed, Juliana. You wanted my son to find it, so he could tell Amelia."

"That's not true," I lied.

"You were my last secret," he chuckled callously. "You actually did me a favor tonight. Here I am thinking of everything I can do to get my wife back knowing I had one more secret I hadn't told her. I didn't have the nerve to tell her. I didn't want to cause her anymore pain to her. I guess my son will deliver that pain to her for me and I will have to deal with the repercussions of my actions."

He looked relieved.

"Thank you," he said. "You have freed me. I never knew how this would feel to have no secrets remaining."

Secrets? What secrets? What was Carson talking about and why was he okay with this?

"You and I are done," he told me. "I will never allow another person to come between me and my wife."

"Baby, you don't mean that."

"Oh yes I do."

He was serious. My heart thundered. This was not how this was supposed to go.

"Baby, let me love you," I pleaded, feeling like this was the last time I was ever going to be with him. With my breath caught in my throat, I held on to the hope Carson would choose me just like I wanted. But an eerie quiet fell between us as we exchanged glances.

"I don't want you. I never wanted you," he asserted.

"You don't mean that."

"Maybe God is allowing all of this to happen because I haven't been the man I should have been."

"You supposed to be with me," I said but he acted like he didn't hear me.

"Here I am, supposed to be a pastor and I'm cheating on the only woman I've ever loved."

Rushing him, I wrapped my arms around his neck saying, "Don't do this to me, Carson. I love you."

"Yeah, you love me enough to sleep, not only with my son-in-law, but also my own son," he retorted. "If you think I can be with you after that, you have lost your mind."

He pried my arms from around him and eased away from me like I had some kind of contagious disease. I was shocked. I couldn't believe Carson was treating me like this.

"You need to leave," he demanded in a bitter tone.

"But…"

"Get out of my house," he said nastily.

I dropped my head in defeat but didn't move.

"I said get out," he roared.

It felt like his voice shook the walls. Tears plunged forward as I backed away from his icy glare.

"This is not over Carson. Not by a long shot."

Skye

My head felt like someone was beating on it with a hammer. The slightest movement caused pain to radiate through my temples. My mouth felt like cotton and breath reeked like never before. It was the next day or at least I hoped so anyway. I wasn't sure. The way I felt, I wasn't sure who I was at this moment. Then it all came rushing back to me. Me drinking and going over to see Seth. Him striking me and getting arrested for it. And Dante coming to pick me up.

I bolted up in bed, causing the room to spin and more throbbing in my temples. Sitting up, or trying to, I grabbed my head. It felt weighted down. Once the room came into focus, I was more confused.

"Where am I?" I whispered, looking around frantically not recognizing the space I was in. This was not my room. This bedroom was painted a soothing blue with white curtains draped at the windows. A thick white comforter hugged me as the pillows played props to my aching body.

I threw back the covers to see I was not in my own clothes.

"Whose clothes is this and who dressed me?" I questioned.

The last thing I remembered was puking my guts out on the side of the road with Dante.

"Dante," I said, eyes widening as I remembered he was who I was with last. Was this his place? Why didn't he take me home?

Throwing my legs over the side of the bed, some fluffy slippers were positioned for me to step into. I smiled thinking whoever took care of me was doing a great job at it. I slid my feet into the slippers and stood to my feet. Immediately, I fell back down on the bed as the room spun.

"Whoa?" I said.

Closing my eyes to gather myself, I stood again, this time getting my balance. I shuffled to the closed door and opened it to see where I was. Laughter greeted me on the other side and I followed the voices. When I turned the corner, two sets of eyes fell upon me. One of a woman and the other set being that of Dante.

"Good morning," he said leaning against the counter in the kitchen as the woman stood at the stove turning bacon she was preparing. She smiled warmly at me.

"Good morning," I groggily said, wondering who this woman was. I know Dante didn't have a girlfriend he didn't tell me about. Not that he had to. I was the one married.

"How do you feel?" he asked.

"I feel like I've been beaten over the head."

"Is this your first hangover?"

"Yes."

"Come on in so I can fix you some coffee. It should help."

I entered the kitchen, watching the woman, put the cooked bacon on a paper towel to soak up the additional grease. She was really pretty. Her natural hair was pulled up atop her head wrapped with an orange, black and red geometric printed scarf. She wore a pair of distressed jean shorts and a tank with a pair of the same fluffy slippers I had on. Dante must've noticed me observing the woman.

"Skye, this is my sister Emery. Emery, this is Skye."

Emery approached me, holding her hand out to shake mine, "It's nice to meet you."

"Same here. I wish it was under better circumstances," I replied feeling ashamed.

"Girl, it's okay. We've all been there," she concluded.

"I haven't," I muttered.

"I brought you to my sister's home because you passed out on me. I didn't know your address, so I thought it was safer to bring you here. I am a man and you were very intoxicated. I didn't want you to think I'd taken advantage of your situation," Dante explained. "My sister is the one who dressed you. You kind of had some vomit on your clothes."

I blushed with embarrassment saying, "I'm so sorry."

"It's okay. I washed your clothes for you. I have them hanging up in the laundry room. I will grab them for you after breakfast," Emery told me.

"I really appreciate this. The both of you have been so accommodating. And Dante, thank you for coming to pick me up."

"It was no problem. After breakfast, I will take you to your car."

The morning was completed with us sitting at the kitchen table eating and the two of them laughing about something that happened in the past. I was in and out of the conversation, a little jealous of their connection. I really had no one who I related to with like that, especially a sibling since I was an only child. The little boy, whom I examined, was in his swing smiling like he knew what his mother and uncle was saying.

After breakfast, I took a shower and got dressed in the same clothes I had on last night. I thanked Emery for her hospitality and rode with Dante to get my car. The tension in the air was thick and that was because of me.

"You've been really quiet. Are you okay?" Dante asked sincerely.

"Honestly, no. These past few days have not been great ones for me."

"Do you mind me asking what happened to your face?"

Reaching up touching the spot Seth struck me at, I said, "My husband hit me."

I looked over to see Dante's jaw clench.

"I was at his mistress house when you picked me up. As you could see, I couldn't drive because I'd been drinking. I went over there to get my husband back."

"Why?" Dante asked.

"Because he's my husband. We supposed to try to make our marriage work."

"It takes two you know."

"I thought if I showed up for him to see how much I cared for him, he would have reconsidered coming home. Little did I know it would lead to being struck and him being arrested for domestic violence?"

"He got what he deserved, and you deserve better," he told me.

"Why would God put me with this man, have me marry him if he wasn't the one for me?"

"How do you know he was the man God meant for you? Sometimes we don't want to see a person is not for us because we are in love with the visual of what it could be, if that makes sense," he stated.

"It does."

"Maybe God has another man for you, a better one."

I gazed over at Dante. He took his eyes off the road for a moment for his eyes to connect with mine. I wanted so badly to ask him was he that man but by then, we were pulling up in front of Fatima's house where he parked behind my ride.

"Thank you Dante, for everything."

"It was my pleasure. But you don't have to get drunk for us to go out with each other. I'm not that bad of a guy that you need to be intoxicated to be with me."

Both of us chuckled.

"You don't have to worry about me getting like this again. Alcohol has become my enemy," I concluded. "I rather be with you with a sober mind."

"Be with?" he asked.

"We already have church tonight. Maybe we can do dinner after?" I suggested.

"I'd like that."

We said our good byes as I got out of his ride to get into my own. He waited patiently watching me make my way to the driver's side. But before I could get into my car, the door to Fatima's home opened and Seth stepped out onto the porch yelling, "Who the heck is that?"

Skye

Seth rushed off the porch and headed towards me. Dante exited his car scowling at him. I held my hand up to stop Dante and he honored my request halting in place.

"Who is he, Skye?" Seth asked in anger.

"He's an old friend of mine."

"Why don't I know about this old friend?" he mocked, glowering at Dante who seemed unfazed by Seth's threatening stance.

"Because we just reconnected. We went to school together."

"And you spent the night with him."

"Not exactly," I muttered.

"Then how was it. Is this why you had me thrown in jail, so you could be with him?"

"I had you arrested because you put your hands on me," I asserted.

"That was after you hit me."

"You put your hands on me first, remember?" I reminded him. "I told you to let me go when you attempted to drag me out of the house, but you refused. I was over here to try to get you back, but you've made it more than clear you are done with me and our marriage," I said with a raised tone.

Seth heaved in a deep breath.

"I don't know why I have to explain anything to you anyway. But since you must know, I was drinking, and I needed a ride because I couldn't drive in the condition I was in. I called Camille, but I didn't get her. So I called Dante."

"And he was more than happy to come scoop you up."

"I sure was," Dante responded.

"Who asked you?" Seth shot back.

"No one important but I decided to speak for myself," Dante retorted.

Moving towards Dante, Seth said, "You have some nerve pulling up to my house with my wife like she's yours."

"Is this your house or your mistress's house?" Dante asked with a frown.

This stunted Seth. He wasn't expecting Dante to know this much about him. I could tell he wasn't happy about that either.

"It seems to me you are confused, partner. Your new woman is right there," Dante pointed to the house where Fatima had emerged from the home. "So, is it Skye you want or her? Make that clear for everyone."

Seth was seething. His fist was clenched tight. The vein in this left temple was pulsating as he gawked at a cool, calm and collected Dante who'd put him on the spot.

"He's right, Seth. Which one of us do you want?"

I said it loud enough for Fatima to hear. Seth was caught between a rock and a hard place. He told me he didn't want me but now that he'd seen me with Dante, he wanted to become territorial.

"I'm not discussing our relationship in front of this punk."

"Oh now it's a relationship?" I questioned.

"I can go sit in the car and wait for you to answer the question for these ladies," Dante suggested as he walked backwards to his ride.

Seth wasn't expecting that, looking distressed he still would have to answer a question he was obviously trying to avoid.

I looked back to see Dante get into his ride and close the door, but he didn't leave. I knew he was staying for me.

Smiling at his generosity, I regretfully turned my attention back to my husband.

"You sleeping with him, Skye?" he interrogated.

Not feeding into his ridiculous ego, I asked, "Who do you choose, Seth? Me or her?"

His frown deepened. Seth shifted his gaze to Fatima who waited impatiently with her arms crossed.

"Go be with your new woman, Seth," I told him.

I opened the door to my car to get in, but Seth gripped the top of the door blocking me.

"Do I need to call the cops on you again?" I threatened.

"I told you I was sorry. I didn't mean to do this to you," he said in a low tone. He reached out to touch my bruised cheek, but I stepped back.

"Apology accepted but I'm done playing these games with you. You've made your choice. So, please, move out of my way so I can leave you two love birds to do whatever it is you do. I have things to do."

"Who? Him. Is he that thing you have to do?"

"If he was what I had to do, that would no longer be your concern, now would it?"

"We are still married, Skye."

"Tell her that. How about you tell yourself that. The divorce papers should be arriving any day, right? Isn't that what you said? I will gladly sign them. I'm done with you."

Seth appeared distraught, even though he was the one who filed for the divorce in the first place.

"Skye," he called out lovingly.

I hadn't heard him say my name like that since the beginning of our relationship. I acknowledged him and waited for him to speak. But when he looked up at the porch to see Fatima giving him a crazed look, he pulled the door open for me to enter.

I shook my head at him and got into my ride closing the door. He walked to the edge of her yard, hands in his pockets watching me drive away with Dante right behind me.

Amelia

Thank heavens I had a restful night's sleep. I had to admit when I woke up, I was a little disoriented and didn't know where I was. I wondered why I didn't hear Carson moving around getting ready to go to the church, but I realized it was because I wasn't home. Then all of the previous day's events came flooding back like a raging river and instantly grief swelled within the pit of my stomach.

"God please help me," I whispered.

The television was still on and some landscaping show was on. I sat up in bed and scooted back to lean against the headboard. I reached over and picked up my phone to turn it back on. Once it was fully booted, my phone buzzed and beeped from the numerous voicemails and text messages I'd received. I couldn't do this now. Not when I woke up feeling pretty good this morning. I was going to take me a hot shower, go down stairs and eat me some breakfast first.

Feeling refreshed, I admired the breakfast options the hotel offered. I was famished and felt like I could sample everything they had. I filled my plate with eggs, sausage, and some fruit. I stood behind this woman who was waiting for her waffle to finish. I wanted one too and figured I would wait my turn to fix one. I didn't have anywhere to be anyway.

As the lady pulled her waffle off the hot skillet, she stepped to the side and said, "There you go."

"Thank you," I responded.

I picked up the plastic cup and filled the mixture to the line. I then poured it into the waffle maker. Closing it, I flipped it and waited for my waffle to cook.

"I would like one of those too," a female voice said.

When I turned, I was surprised to see Elaine standing behind me with her arms folded across her chest. I immediately searched to see if anyone else was with her.

"I'm by myself," she told me.

"How did you know I was here?"

"We are best friends aren't we? You thought I would forget about the conversation we had way back if we ever needed to get away and go somewhere to be by ourselves, we would come to this hotel."

I smiled, remembering the conversation. The waffle maker beeped letting me know my waffle was done and I retrieved it from the hot skillet to put on the plate with the rest of my food.

After Elaine fixed herself a plating knowing she was not a paying customer at this hotel, we both went back to my hotel room instead of sitting in the allotted spaces in the area to eat.

Sitting on the bed with her plate of food which was stacked higher than mine, she said, "You had me sitting down in that lobby for an hour. Be happy with the staff because they refused to tell me what room you were in. Did you give them our fake name?" she asked.

"Yes I used Monica Prillaman," I said.

"Okay, Monica," she joked, "Tell me what's going on."

"It's a long story, Elaine."

"I got all day. Speak Ms. Thang."

"Can I at least eat first?" I laughed.

"You can eat and talk at the same time like I'm doing," she muttered with a mouth full of waffles.

Sitting Indian style, I took a bite of my sausage I said, "It's bad, Elaine. Real bad."

"I figured that when Carson called me. Then Aden called me. And even Payton called looking for you. All of them are worried sick about you. So is your brother. He was ready to call the police and have a missing person's report filed on you."

I giggled at my friend knowing she was serious. My brother was protective over me. His over baring ways use to get on my nerve but now I loved him for it.

"You didn't answer your phone. It kept going straight to voicemail which let me know you turned your phone off."

"Carson didn't mention what was going on?" I asked tersely.

"Not at all. You know I asked but he told me the two of you were having some difficulties."

"That's stating it lightly."

"It can't be that bad, Amelia."

Swallowing the waffle I just put into my mouth, I said, "It's bad enough for me to consider asking Carson for a divorce."

"What?" Elaine blurted in shock. "Amelia, no. You two are made for each other."

"Were made for each other."

"That man loves you."

I began to explain the entire tumultuous day to her and when I was done, Elaine was looking at me stunned.

"I don't even know what to say."

"What is there to say?" I responded.

"So how does Aden fit into all of this?"

"What do you mean?" I asked frowning.

"Girl, Aden called me crying."

"What?" I asked with worry.

"Yes. He was very upset he couldn't hardly speak. He just kept asking where you were, saying he needed to talk to you and that it was urgent. He didn't sound okay at all. Did he leave you a message?"

"I haven't checked. I figured most of my messages were from Carson."

"Girl, get your phone so we can see what's going on," she coaxed.

I did what Elaine said suggested and checked my text messages first. I'd received fourteen from Carson pleading with me to forgive him and come home to talk about everything. I received a couple from Elaine and Diego. I had eight from my daughter Payton wondering where I was and that she was worried and to call her. And I had seventeen from Aden to get in touch with him as soon as possible. The voicemails left were much of the same.

"These still don't tell me what the urgency is," I said, feeling uneasy.

"Call Carson and talk to him," Elaine said.

"I'm not ready to talk to him yet."

"Then call Aden. Maybe he knows something."

Dialing Aden's number, I waited for him to answer.

"Mom," he belted into the phone.

"Hey sweetie."

"Where are you? Are you okay?" he forced out.

"I'm fine. I'm staying at a hotel. I needed some time to myself."

"Mom," he paused. A silence fell between us.

"Aden, honey. What's wrong?" I asked worriedly.

"It's bad mom. It's really bad," he broke down.

My stomach churned. What could be so bad that my son was in tears like this.

"I really need you mom. I need to talk to you. Can I come see you?"

I gave Aden the location where I was wondering what else was going on. Did Juliana hurt my baby? Did she have anything to do with this? There was nothing left for me to do but pray, which I did with Elaine. I asked her to stick around just in case I needed her. She happily obliged and I was grateful because I wasn't sure if I was strong enough to handle anything else.

Amelia

When I heard the knock at the door, my stomach lurched with emotions. I sat on the bed, not able to move and watched as Elaine scurried to the door to open it. I heard her gasp when she saw him. When he entered, that's when I saw why.

Rushing over to him, I asked, "What happened to you?"

Aden had a black eye, swollen nose, and busted lip. I gently touched his wounded face upset by his appearance.

"Dad happened," he blurted angrily as he moved out of my grasp and walked pass me. He made his way to the window where he looked out at the city view, but he didn't say anything. This worried me.

I cut my eye at Elaine. She hunched her shoulders looking just as confused as I did.

"Son, tell me what's going on. Why would your father do this to you?"

He pivoted around to face me and said, "Mom, I think you should sit down."

As if my stomach wasn't torn up enough, it tightened even more. Unknowingly, I placed my hand on

274

it to stop the uncomfortable feeling. If Aden was asking me to sit down, I knew whatever he was about to tell me was going to be unpleasant. If his face was any indication of how bad, this news could be devastating. I shifted my gaze to Elaine who was looking intently at us. Both Elaine and I lowered ourselves on the bed waiting for Aden to speak. When he took a long moment, I made it a point to break the silence.

"Tell me why you and your father got into a fight. Did you find out everything?" I asked, thinking he found out the truth about his dad's true identity or maybe his intimate connection with a man.

"Find out what?" Aden asked puzzled.

"Just tell me, Aden, what is so urgent, honey."

I could tell by the baffled expression he didn't know what I was talking about and I wasn't about to disclose this information to him.

"No mom. You tell me what you are talking about," he said forcefully. "It's a reason why you are in this room and not at home like you should be."

"Amelia, maybe you should tell him. He's going to find out sooner or later anyway," Elaine proposed.

"Find out what?" he asked rigidly.

Sighing, I said, "Yesterday I found out your dad is not who he claims to be."

"What does that mean?" Aden asked with a scowl.

"Your dad's name is not Carson. It's Benjamin."

"What?"

"Your dad took on his brother's identity and—"

Interrupting, he asked with confusion etched on his face, "I don't understand. Are you trying to tell me my dad isn't my dad?"

"Carson is your father, but his name isn't really Carson."

Without warning, Aden punched the wall putting a hole the size of his fist in it.

"Aden," I yelled.

"Who is this man? He's been lying to you, to me, to Payton, to everybody all these years."

With my son being as angry as he was, I didn't think it was wise to disclose the rest of the information to him.

"Sweetie, you need to calm down."

"Mom, you don't understand," he said with water welling up in his eyes. "Dad…Dad. Dad…" he kept saying not able to complete his sentenced.

"What?"

My son rushed over to me dropping to his knees. He flung his arms around me, collapsing in my embrace where I held him tenderly. Seeing my son in pain like this caused me to want to break down but I knew I couldn't. I look to Elaine who was still in the dark like I was, not knowing where the root of my son's anguish was coming from.

"Mom, I don't want you to hurt anymore," Aden said weeping like he was four years old again.

"Son, I'm going to be okay. You can tell me anything."

"I know mom but how much more can you handle," he said looking up into my eyes. He was gauging my emotions. He wanted to see if I was lying or telling him the truth.

I smiled sincerely, cupping his face, letting him know it was okay. Aden nodded leaning his face back into my stomach.

"Dad. Dad has been cheating on you," Aden finally divulged.

I looked up to the ceiling whispering *Jesus* in my mind as I waited for my son to continue.

"He's been cheating on you with…with Juliana."

Amelia

It was our second night of revival and despite what was going on in my life, I still had a position to play as first lady. If I couldn't be a leader as the first lady here and show people how to rise above whatever you are going through to attend church, then I felt like I would be failing them. No, I was failing me. I needed to be here for me as well.

I didn't bother to go see Carson, not after what my son revealed to me. My husband was cheating on me with Juliana, the same woman who'd been sleeping with our son. You would think when she came over that day after church, my husband would have spoken up, even if it was only to get our child away from that crazed woman. It was obvious she was trying to get back at him in the worst way and he allowed that woman to use our child to do it. Here I was thinking I should keep Juliana away from Aden when she'd already had my husband. But that was okay. After tonight, everything would be over.

The pianist began to play, letting the members know it was time to be seated because the service was about to start. A few of the ministers sat in the pulpit but I had yet to lay eyes on Carson. When I looked in the choir stand, my son sat there looking miserable. I was surprised he even showed. Despite some major pleading from him for us not to attend church tonight, I told him I had to go. Explaining to him my reasons why, he finally gave in and got comfortable with me coming. He insisted on coming with me, bruised up and all. I was proud of him. He came for me, I knew this. He wanted to make sure I was safe and despite everything that transpired, he kept is obligation to this church to do his role as the director of this choir. Payton sat in the choir also, looking confused. After Aden and Elaine left my hotel room, I made it a point to call my daughter to let her know I was okay. She didn't believe me, especially since I wasn't at home. But I reassured her I was. I knew after seeing her brother's face, she knew okay was far from the truth.

Payton gazed at me and I smiled back at my beautiful daughter. She returned the gesture smiling weakly. I hated we'd kept her in the dark, but I wanted to spare her the torment for as long as I could. It was bad enough seeing my son in the pain he was in. I definitely didn't want to see my daughter in that same pain, especially since she was a daddy's girl. Carson was everything to her. He was a wonderful father to our children, I couldn't deny that. This was why this was so hard to believe all the secrets that were coming to light.

Carson finally entered the pulpit, making it a point to look in my direction to see if I was here. His expression was that of surprise when he saw me. He flashed me that smile I fell in love with, but I glared at him. I wanted him to see nothing had changed between us. If anything, things were worse.

Skye walked up beside me. She grinned down at me, so she could sit beside me. She looked different to me, stronger. I was curious what changed for her.

Carson approached the podium and began to speak to the congregation.

"Good evening church."

Everyone spoke in unison. I saw Aden grimace at his dad. It was clear Carson got the upper hand on our son in their altercation because he didn't look like he had a scratch on him.

"It's good to be in the house of the Lord one more time," Carson said.

"Amen," some members agreed.

"Last night, we had an amazing time, didn't we? Carson asked, and the congregation shouted their approval. All but me.

"I preached about the Christian woman and how difficult it is for the Christian woman to try to maintain her faith and walk in the word without falling into the traps of the devil."

"Say so, pastor," someone shouted.

"Children, marriage, and just plain being the woman God intended her to be is a challenge for some if not all women. So tonight, it is only fair that I speak on the subject of the Christian man," he said proudly.

I wanted to vomit. Was Carson serious? The Christian man. Was he about to confess his sins in front of the congregation because I didn't think it was proper for him to play with God like this? If he kept it up, Jesus was going to come down from the heavens and render my husband the ultimate wrath which could end in death.

"But before I began my sermon, we are going to ask our amazing choir to uplift us with a song of praise."

Carson turned towards the choir, no doubt looking at our son. Aden ignored him but got up to face the choir as he signaled the pianist to start playing the tunes to the song, *Too Hard Not to* by Tina Campbell. As soon as the tune started, I watched my daughter stepped forward to the microphone. I knew this was going to be a moment of tears for me. This song couldn't be more fitting for what I was going through right now. I stood without hesitation raising my hand in the air. By the end of that song, the entire church was on their feet, including Skye lifting God's name up to the heavens. And when the choir followed that song with *Break Every Chain by* Tasha Cobbs, the church didn't bother to sit down as my daughter put her soul into this song. Tears continued to plunge forward as the music comforted me. The place was filled with the Holy spirit. People were shouting and dancing like never before. Even Skye got so filled up with the spirit that she was in the aisle screaming, "Jesus!" over and over again. The entire room was breathless with praise when the song ended. It wasn't until everybody gathered themselves enough to sit back down that I saw Juliana sitting at the other end of the pew.

I couldn't believe her nerve. Not only did she have the audacity to show her face here tonight, but she still had the bravado to sit her Jezebel behind on the same pew as me. Instantly, I began to tremble as rage took over me. It was just like the devil to walk right up in here and snatch my peace away. I always felt like I could control myself but in this moment, I was on the verge of letting this church see another side of me that wasn't going to be God like.

I closed my eyes and prayed to the Lord to intervene because I knew he knew my heart. He knew it was taking everything in me not to walk over to this woman and punch her dead in her face.

"Mrs. Reid, are you okay?" Skye asked jerking me out of my prayer.

"No, not really," I answered truthfully. "I think I need to get up and get some water," I told her, thinking of anything to remove myself from the situation before I did something I regretted.

"I'll go with you," Skye said getting up and waiting for me to stand to step out in the aisle. I glanced at Carson and saw the look of dismay on his face. He saw her too and looked gray with worry knowing this was not a good situation.

I left the sanctuary to enter the vestibule with Skye walking closely behind me. When I was free from prying eyes, I paced the area and wondered if I could go back in the church.

"You don't have to stay out here with me, Skye. Go back inside and enjoy the service," I told her, really needing to be alone right now.

"I can stay," she said looking at me with concern. "I feel like I should."

Her face was etched with worry, eyes troubled and I walked over to her.

"I'm okay, sweetie. I just need a minute to myself. Go back inside," I insisted gripping her hand comfortingly. "If I'm not back in there in a few minutes, you can come check on me."

Skye smiled thinly with uncertainty evident on her face. But she did as I asked and entered the sanctuary leaving me to myself.

I collapsed in the available chair and breathed hard as I struggled to control my anger. My chest felt like a ten ton elephant was sitting on it and I wondered was I on the verge of having a panic attack.

"Please, God help me," I begged.

As if the devil knew to kick me when I was down, the door to the church swung open and out walked Juliana herself looking as proud as she wanted to be.

With a wicked grin, she asked, "Are you okay?"

Trying not to curse up in this church, I again pleaded with God to intervene on my behalf.

"I know you are a whole lot older than me, but I didn't think you had trouble with your hearing," she taunted.

Blowing out a breath, I said, "I think it's best you leave me alone."

"Come on, First Lady. Is that any way to treat your future daughter-in-law?"

My eyes widen with fury .

"Or I guess I could be the next First Lady in line at this church. First Lady Juliana Simmons. I like the way that sounds," she provoked.

"I already know about your torrid affair with Carson," I informed her.

"So Aden had the nerve to tell you? Good. That's what I counted on," she said cockily. "I don't know what Carson was waiting for. He told me he was going to ask you for a divorce. He took too long though."

"*Submit yourselves, then, to God. Resist the devil and he will flee from you,*" I quoted James 4:8.

"That's why I had to take matters into my own hands to speed things up."

"The God of peace will soon crush Satan under your feet. The grace of our Lord Jesus be with you," I recited Roman 16:20.

"Too bad Aden caught that beat down. I don't know why he thought he could whoop Carson's behind. It's obvious his father is more of a man than he is."

Blind rage surged through me, but I maintained my composure. I was in the house of the Lord.

Jesus, I mentally called him again in my mind.

Juliana continued.

"It would be wise for you not to fight this because Carson doesn't want to be married to you anymore. There is a reason why he came to me. I guess you weren't giving him what he needed. But I made sure to give it to him and your son real good."

I jumped up and rushed Juliana. She didn't see me coming as I grabbed a handful of her hair and yanked her to the floor. She tumbled hard. I pounced on her, never letting my grip go as I used her hair to pull her face into each blow from my fist. I wanted this woman to hurt like I'd been hurting, whether it was mentally or physically. Right now, physically would have to do. Plus, it made me feel better as I pommeled her mercilessly.

Skye

I heard the screams inside the church and instantly thought about Mrs. Reid. I got up from the pew and bolted to the vestibule in a panic. A few members followed, also wondering what was going on. But what I saw, I wasn't expecting to see. First Lady Reid had Juliana on the floor punching her in the face.

"Mrs. Reid, no," I yelled rushing over to pull her off of Juliana.

As I struggled to get her away, Mrs. Reid continued to delivery blows and kicks to a helpless Juliana.

Aden appeared, along with Pastor Reid and a few other church members who were being noisy.

"Mom, stop," Aden cried out trying to unwind Mrs. Reid fingers from around Juliana's clothing. All of us struggled to get them two apart, which was a feat that seemed impossible. Mrs. Reid was a lot stronger than she appeared but eventually we were able to separate them.

I'd never seen Mrs. Reid so angry in my life. She'd checked out. Her focus was on Juliana and she was vying to get her hands back on her.

"Mom, it's me, Aden," her son said, trying to get Mrs. Reid to calm down.

"Get that home wrecker out of this church now!" Mrs. Reid roared.

"You better tell her Carson. Tell her you don't want to be with her and you want to be with me," Juliana belted from the floor.

"You heard, Amelia. Get out of this church, Juliana," Carson shouted.

"You are taking her side. After everything I've done for you. After all the love I've giving you," Juliana exclaimed as she struggled to get up from the floor. "You told me she can't please you like I can."

The moans and whispers going on around us sounded like a bee hive being disturbed. The buzz was on. I scanned the space to see many of the parishioners watching in astonishment at this display of the devils work at its best.

One of the elder deacons walked up to Pastor Reid and asked him, "Pastor, is this true? Have you been seeing this woman?"

In that instance, the buzzing stopped as the church fell silent. Everyone waited with baited breath for him to answer. You couldn't hear anything, not even people breathing as everyone stared pointedly at the pastor waiting for him to speak.

"Tell him, Carson. Tell him you love me, and we've been sleeping together for the past eight month."

"Lord, Jesus help us Lord," a woman muttered with a grimace.

"Daddy," Payton called out as she made her way through the crowd. "Please tell them this is not true? Please tell these people you haven't been cheating on our mother."

You could see the hope in his daughter's eyes. She waited for him to respond but her father had no words. He surveyed the area and was silenced by the question, which, to me, was answer enough.

Speaking up for them, I said, "Everyone, as you can see this has been a big misunderstanding. Yes, this event is unfortunate, but we need to respect the First Lady and the pastor's privacy."

"Who cares about them?" Juliana belted. "What about me?"

"Be quiet," Aden told her.

"Everyone deserves to know the truth," Juliana continued.

"Yes they do," another person said. Everyone looked around to see where that statement came from. "Tell them, Carson," Delilah said parting the crowd as she approached.

Wasn't she his sister? Why would she side with Juliana, I wondered?

"Your members deserve the truth and nothing, but the truth so help you God."

She smirked wickedly at her brother who stood frozen in place. His face was absent of emotion as he gaped at his sister.

"Tell them how you are not who you say you are."

I was expecting Mrs. Reid to come to the defense of her husband even after she'd beaten Juliana down, but she was rooted in place. Aden was holding her in his arms and Payton joined them. She posted up on the other side of her mother looking as though her and her brother were attempting to shield their mother from all this drama. I'd never seen Mrs. Reid looked so defeated. She didn't have an ounce of fight left which meant Pastor Reid was on his own.

"Dee Dee, leave this alone," Carson pleaded.

"Ladies and gentlemen, let me introduce you to Benjamin Reid."

Confusion gripped the faces of many as they looked around to see who his sister was talking about.

"No need to look around because he's standing in front of you," she said gesturing towards Pastor Reid.

"What is she talking about?" Payton whimpered.

"This is my brother Benjamin. Not Carson Reid. Benjamin took on our deceased brother's identity years ago and has been living his life under our brother's name."

"I'm finding me another, church," a member blurted.

"This is better than the *Young and the Restless*," another said.

"More like the *Bold and the Beautiful*," another quipped.

"This world is going straight to where the devil resides, you hear me," an elder member added.

I thought all of these things. The life I thought I understood was clouded with deceit and lies. This man had been my minister for years. He married Seth and I.

"He's not a minister either," Mrs. Reid finally spoke.

"What?" Aden questioned, letting go of his mother as he gaped at her in confusion. Payton, along with many others watched intently as Mrs. Reid continued.

"I found all of this out last night," she said in a subdued pitch.

"You knew and didn't say anything," I asked in annoyance.

"I didn't know what to do. I left my home to stay at a hotel to wrap my mind around this. I was upset, confused, and couldn't figure out how to handle this information. Then I found out today about him and Juliana sleeping together. My life has been a fraud for all these years because this man decided to play with my life for the comfort of his own," Mrs. Reid said flatly.

"So if you are not a minster, then that means I'm not married," I said with the realization not only was their marriage a fraud but mine was not legal either.

The church began to rumble as the absorption of the revelations smacked everybody in the face leaving a nasty taste in each of our mouths.

"He still can preach," someone defended.

"That he can. You got real ministers out here not preaching the word like he does," another said.

I didn't care to hear anyone else's opinion on this matter because now my life had taken another turn in the wrong direction. I'd had enough. I needed to gather my purse and get out of here as soon as possible. I rushed through the thickness of the crowd and entered the church to retrieve my purse. But when I went to the pew I was sitting at, I didn't see it.

Someone touched my shoulder and I whirled around to see Dante. And he was holding my purse.

Juliana

I tried jerking out of the grasp of two church member who were holding on to me. One of them was Deacon Dwight. Bastard. I swear if I really wanted to I could expose most of the men in this church. I surveyed everyone who gawked at me in judgment. Some looked at me with pity and some in disgust. I even saw some members pulling their husband close to them like I was going to go after their man next. Little did some of them know I'd had a lot of them? Some of these men held a position in this church trying to appear to be living the Christian life when the majority of them were living a lie. Carson just happened to be the one whose transgressions were exposed.

So as I stood here, beat up by his stuck-up wife who was playing the victim after she assaulted me. I waited for Carson to come to my defense but he didn't. My only saving grace was his sister. From the looks of things, she too had a score to settle with Carson and his wife. I wasn't sure what that was, but I really didn't care. She was helping me with my situation. More dirt being brought up only made what I was saying look true.

Fed up with the eye rolls and whispers, I shouted, "What are y'all looking at? You've never seen a woman hurt by a man before. Or maybe you haven't seen a woman hurt by a married minister before."

"That girl is crazy," a member commented.

"Shut up you old hag. You jealous because I'm young, tender and wanted. Your time has passed. You need to keep your mouth shut before you find someone to shut it for you."

The woman gasped.

"Enough," Deacon Dwight said.

"I don't think you want to be talking to me like that, Deacon," I warned.

I gave him a look that made him shift uncomfortably. He knew to keep his mouth shut when it came to dealing with me. I hadn't slept with him, but I found other ways to please his Vienna sausage. I searched the room and found his wife's eyes on me too. Her eyes darted back and forth between the Deacon and me. She appeared nervous, like I was going to start announcing other men I'd been with in this sanctum. Maybe I should. Maybe I should put all of them on blast. That would teach all of these Holy rollers everything wasn't perfect as much as they tried to pretend. It was a lot of secrets within these walls and I held fifty percent of them.

I was snapped out of my thoughts when Carson approached me. He grabbed me by the arm and began pulling me out of the vestibule and into the darkness of the night.

"Why are you doing this to me?" I asked sincerely.

Pushing me outside and letting the doors close behind him and I, I could see through the transparent glass the church members moving around. Some were still watching to see what was going to happen, but many took this as their queue to leave.

"We are over," Carson snarled.

"I know you are not going back to your wife?" I expressed.

"If Amelia is gracious enough to take me back, then yes, I'm going back. I'm going to run to her because she is the woman I love. There is no woman who will ever take her place."

"You don't mean that."

"Oh yes I do. I may lose everything because I haven't done right by my wife, my children, this church or God. But that's fine with me because I'm free. I'm free of you. I'm free of my sister and I'm free of these secrets. And now that I'm free, I'm never having anything to do with you again."

Carson spoke soft and calm. No anger came from him and this bothered me. He turned his back on me and walked back into the sanctuary.

Yelling, I said, "Please don't do this to me, Carson. Please!"

My words fell on death ears.

I ran to the door to enter the sanctuary again, but it was blocked by some Deacons who refused to allow me back in. Carson disappeared into the crowd of people. I was devastated. Things couldn't end like this. Not with me not getting what I wanted. I was a faithful servant who served many, but I was loyal to Carson. How could he turn his back on me like this? That was okay. If it was the last thing I did, I was going to make them all pay, and this entire church was going to remember who Juliana Simmons is.

Amelia

I laid in the bed in the hotel room and cried my eyes out. I cried because I was hurt. I cried because I was embarrassed. And I cried because I let the devil step in and allow me to disrespect God's house. How could I be so stupid? How could I let the devil get the best of me like this? I was better than that, yet I back slid in a major way allowing everyone to see me out of my character. I wondered if I could ever get pass this. And would the congregation forgive me for what I'd done? Will they think I played a part in Carson's fraud?

"Mom, would you like something to drink?" Aden asked approaching my bed.

I swiped at the tears that were quickly soaking my pillow.

"I'm good," I struggled to say.

Aden sat down on the side of the bed next to me and placed a comforting hand on my back.

"Mom, I'm so sorry for all of this. You, of all people, don't deserve any of this."

"You do not have to apologize. None of this is your fault."

"I feel like it is. I brought Juliana into our lives and in our home. You were right about her. You warned me, but I thought you were being over baring. I should have listened to you," he said dropping his head.

Reaching over, I lifted his chin for his eyes to meet mine.

"Honey, you didn't know any of this when you got with her."

"She was using me, and you saw that."

"Both of us were fooled by her and Carson."

"Don't you mean Benjamin?" he drawled.

"Right now, he's Carson to me. That's who I've known, loved, married, and had children with, even if it was a lie."

"Please tell me you are going to divorce him," Aden said.

"Honey, I don't know."

"Even after what has happened, you don't know?" he questioned.

"I don't. My mother use to tell me never make a move mad. And trust me, I'm angry. Now is not the time for me to make a rash decision."

"But he's a fraud and a cheater."

"This is true. Still, I'm going to have to pray on this situation."

"Where was God when all of this happened? Where was God when he allowed this man to enter your life to later pull the rug from under you? He's made you look like a fool."

"Hold up, son," I stopped him. "First of all, don't talk down about God like that. What you need to understand *God is our refuge and strength, a very present help in trouble.* Psalm 46:1."

"He allowed this. How is he our refuge? Did he see this coming? Couldn't he stop this from happening?"

"Every negative thing that happens has a lesson we need to learn," I said.

"What is there to learn here, how not to trust people? How not to love?" Aden frowned.

My son was angry, and I understood why. I'd been where he was many times. I'm not quite sure when that shift happened for me.

"Aden, you are going to have to forgive in order to move on. For we have all sin and fall short of the glory of God. A sin is a sin, is a sin. Even as the first lady, I've been sinning every day. This situation could have happened to teach me a lesson about myself. There is a lesson here for all of us. We just have to seek and find what that is," I explained.

I wasn't sure if I was getting through to my son, but I had to try. There was no way I could have him blaming God for this situation.

"Aden, honey. Look at me. I'm still standing. I'm going to be fine."

"But you are crying. I hate to see you in pain like this," he said gloomily.

"I'm just relieving some pressure that's built up over the past couple of days. Don't worry about me because your mother is going to bounce back like a champ. *No weapons formed against me shall prosper*," I said smiling at my son.

He weakly smiled back at me.

"I love you, baby."

"I love you too, mom."

A knock at the door interrupted me and my son's conversation.

"I'm getting rid of whoever that is," Aden told me as he rose from the bed and went to the door. When he opened it, I could feel the mood in the room change, and not for the good.

"Who is it, Aden?" I asked.

"It's nobody," he answered coldly.

"It's me, Amelia."

It was Carson.

"How dare you show your face here after what you've done?" Aden said sharply.

"Son…"

"Don't son me. I'm no son of yours, Benjamin."

Climbing out of the bed to go to the door, I saw Carson drop his head as his hands rested in the pockets of his black slacks. Carson looked hurt by Aden calling him by his government name. His disappointment was evident, especially in himself and he knew he deserved how Aden was treating him.

"Aden, let him in."

"Mom!" Aden objected.

"It's okay, sweetie."

Aden hesitated for a moment glaring at his father but eventually stepped back to allow Carson to enter.

"Son, give your father and I a moment."

"I'm not leaving you alone with him," Aden rejected.

"I will be fine. Go grab you something to eat and check on Payton while you at it. I'll call you if I need you, okay," I said with sincere eyes.

Aden walked over to me and planted a kiss on my cheek. I patted his arm and watched as he brushed pass Carson, shoulder checking him as he exited the room. Carson didn't say anything, but he did look upset at the fact Aden was blatantly disrespecting him. I didn't condone it either, but I understood. I made a mental note to talk to my son about that later. But for now, I had to deal with the man who I'd spent a quarter of my life with.

"What do you want, Carson?" I asked smoothly.

"You've been crying," he surmised.

I let out a chuckle saying, "What do you expect? It was either this or hurt someone."

"I hate to see you cry."

"Then you shouldn't have given me any reasons to."

Carson nodded.

"How did you know I was here?" I asked.

"Elaine told me. And please, don't be mad at her. I explained to her how I wanted to apologize for everything that happened. I didn't mean for any of this to come about."

"Are you talking about lying to me for twenty-five years? Are you talking about lying to the church about not being a legit minister? Or are you talking about sleeping with Juliana?" I asked heartlessly.

"I'm apologizing for all of it. I've ruined so many lives but the lives that matter the most to me are you and my children."

"It's a little late to care, don't you think?"

"It's never too late. I'm a living witness, even if I used my deceased brother's name to move on. The name was a name but the man holding that name is another thing."

"You did what you wanted to do without thinking about how it would affect others. Your lies have created a firestorm of turmoil," I told him.

"I never meant—"

Interrupting him I said, "Don't you dare say you never meant for any of this to happen. You may have lied about your name and about being a pastor, but you also cheated on me, Carson, with a woman who used your son. She slept with him to get back at you. I bet you never thought that was going to happen. But most men don't think of the consequences of their actions when they stick their—"

"Amelia," he stopped me.

Pressing my lips together, I sighed deeply.

"That was the one thing I thought you would never do to me."

"I'm sorry. I will say it a thousand times for a thousand days if it means getting you back in my life again," he pleaded.

"It's too late."

Carson stepped forward, but I held up a hand for him not to come any closer.

"Please, Amelia. Don't do this. Not now."

"If not now, then when?"

"I…I don't know," he stuttered.

"Am I supposed to be the loving wife who stands by her husband's side even after his betrayal?"

He didn't answer but I could tell that's exactly what he wanted me to do.

I shook my head as I chuckled again.

"You must think I'm one of those politician wives who stand in the midst of scandal and hold her head up high beside the man who destroyed her. You've been with me long enough to know that's not me. Trust is the foundation of a marriage including love. You have disregarded both of those essential elements. I'm not willing to do another twenty-five years trying to rebuild with a man I don't even know or trust."

"But, I love you."

"I'm not sure what your definition of love is but sleeping with another woman doesn't quite fall in the realms of love to me."

He nodded again. A brief silence fell between us before he spoke again.

"Can you please wait to file divorce papers after we have our meeting with the board of trustees at church?" he asked dejectedly.

"I can't promise you that," I said earnestly.

"Are you coming to the meeting after the revival service Friday night?"

"I'm not sure yet," I answered. I wasn't sure I wanted to face anyone after what happened. I knew the meeting was to throw Carson and myself out of the church to save it somehow.

"If you can come, Amelia, please do."

I nodded.

"I'm not going to give up on us. If you need anything, please call me."

I didn't respond. Carson got the hint this conversation was done. Hesitantly, he made his way to the door. He took a long gaze back at me before exiting the room. I drew in a deep breath, feeling like I was holding it the entire time he was here. Internally, I struggled with if I was making the right decision about my marriage. My pride said leave him, but my heart said this man loved me. I still loved him. He made a mistake. Who hasn't? Still, too much had happened. Each time I asked him if there was anything else, he lied by not saying anything. What if there was something else he was holding from me again. I was torn. I wasn't sure if I was willing to take that chance on getting my heart broken again.

Skye

Seth was, of course, hesitant about coming over but eventually agreed when I told him it was urgent. I even told him if he wanted to bring Fatima with him, he could. I didn't want her thinking I was trying to get back with him and I didn't want him thinking I was threatened by her. He made his choice and I'd accepted his decision. To my surprise Seth showed up alone. He looked around like he was expecting things to have changed after his leaving. He looked around and examined the space like it was his first time in it. The only change in this room was us.

"Thank you for coming over," I said gesturing for him to have a seat. I joined him, sitting on the opposite end of the sofa. He looked handsome in a pair of his slacks and a button-down shirt. I would be lying to myself if I didn't admit I still loved him. That wouldn't go away so easily.

"You said it was urgent. You've never used that word before," he said sincerely.

"I wanted to talk to you about us."

An unsettled expression covered his face.

"Wait. I understand you don't want to be with me anymore," I said trying to explain. "This is not what this conversation is about. I think the two of us made it perfectly clear where we stood, correct?" I asked.

He nodded in agreement. I could see his demeanor relax a bit when I said that. I didn't want him to think this was going to be another knock down drag out conversation about how we could make this work.

"I had you come over to tell you I'm not giving you a divorce."

"But, you just said—"

"Let me finish," I cut him off. "The reason why I'm not giving you a divorce is because we are not legally married."

Seth's brows bunched in confusion. He asked, "What are you talking about, we are not legally married?"

Biting the corner of my lip I continued.

"I found out last night Pastor Reid is not a legally practicing minister. So when he performed our wedding, he basically committed fraud against us because he's a fraud."

"What?" he groaned.

"I'm just as shocked as you are. I don't know whether to be happy because this will save us the time and effort regarding a divorce or sad because I ended up giving myself to you anyway without the bond of marriage," I said despondently.

"Is that all you care about, losing your virginity without being married?" he snipped.

"That was important me, Seth. I thought you knew that."

"I did but there are bigger things to be concerned with here. We are not married. We've never been married."

"Why are you getting upset about it?" I asked perplexed. "Isn't this what you wanted?"

"Yes. No. Look, Skye, I don't know."

"What do you mean you don't know? You've told me on several occasions we were a mistake and you didn't love me the way I deserved. I thought you would be happy to hear this news."

"I am."

"Then good" I said standing. I wanted this discussion to end because it took too much energy for me to have this conversation in the first place.

Null and Void

Seth looked up at me with a befuddled expression I didn't understand. I walked around him and went to the door.

"Thank you for coming over," I said reaching for the door. This was his queue to leave.

"Skye, I made a mistake," he blurted.

Turning to face him, his head was hung low.

"About what?"

"You. Us. Our marriage."

"There is no marriage," I said.

Sighing, he muttered, "I know that now."

"Then what's the problem?"

Reluctantly, he asked, "Do you love him?"

"Love who?" I inquired.

"That dude you were with the other day."

I nodded, tongue in cheek knowing what this was about.

"You're jealous," I surmised.

"It's just? When I saw you with him, it did something to me," he said bawling his fist.

"What? You didn't think another man would want me?"

309

"No."

I reached for the door knob and Seth rose quickly from the sofa darting in my direction. He gripped my arm and I jerked it away from him hoping this was not going to be another repeat of him thinking it was okay to put his hands on me.

He held his hands up in surrender, letting me know he wasn't trying to hurt me.

"I didn't mean what I said."

"Then what did you mean, Seth?"

"I didn't think you would find someone so soon."

"You did. Isn't that how you and Fatima's relationship got started, through a brief encounter. At least I knew Dante. He was a guy I went to school with, nothing more. I haven't slept with him or kissed him. He is an old friend who happen to be here for me, unlike you."

His jaw clenched.

"I made a mistake, Skye."

"Well it's one you are going to have to learn to live with because what you and I had is done," I said with finality.

"Don't say that," he pleaded.

"I may not be as experienced as you are, but I am smart, smart enough to know to believe a person when they show you who they really are. Thank you for showing me who you really are. I can move on just like you did. Now, I did you a favor by disclosing this information about our marriage to you. As far as I'm concerned, our business together is finished. You can go be with your little side piece and leave me alone to do me now."

I opened the door and stepped to the side for him to exit. He hesitated, looking at me with sad eyes but I didn't care.

"I love you, Skye," he said trudging pass me to leave.

"I love you too, but I love myself more."

With those final words, I slammed the door behind him.

Amelia

It was Friday night and my stomach was churning with the anticipation of walking into the church tonight. I hadn't stepped foot inside the sanctuary since the night I jumped on Juliana but knew I wanted to be there to support the guest pastor who was visiting from Maryland to preach tonight. I asked the board could I speak tonight, and they gladly agreed it would be okay. I needed to address the church even if for a moment.

The only communication I had with anyone was with my children, my brother, and Elaine. Everyone else, I shut out to clear my mind and use that time to pray and seek God on how to move forward in my life.

I looked at myself in the mirror and stared into my own eyes. I knew I could do this. I was not a woman who bowed down to no one. So, today I was going to hold my head high, walk in that church, and take my seat in the pew I'd sat in for years now.

I had yet to return home. Carson called every day asking me to come home, but I couldn't. Not yet. I did miss my home though. I missed my bed, my kitchen and my jetted soaking tub. There was nothing like being in your own, but I had to take this time for me. Aden came by every day checking on me. He's been by my side this entire ordeal. He wanted to stay in the room with me, but I told that boy absolutely not. He needed to go home to his own place and let me do me. I did give him a key to my room. I did the same for Payton. She was really having a difficult time with things. I hated to see my kids in pain like this. The only thing I could do was love them through this storm.

Elaine and my brother Diego have been by to check on me also. My brother was rightfully upset about everything that happened. He and Carson had a very close bond. They ended up speaking with each other about everything, but I was not witness to that conversation, nor did I want to be. Whatever they talked about was between them. If Diego wanted to continue to be great friends with Carson, I wouldn't have a problem with that. I was not going to be that person that if the marriage didn't work out, my family would have to cut all ties with him. I wasn't that cold.

I walked over to my bed and picked up my mint colored organza hat with a frilly ruffled brim. It was beautifully accented with soft flowers, feathers, and rhinestones. I admired the beauty of the piece and placed it on my head. Walking over to the full length mirror, I stood knowing I looked good. This mint colored two piece suit and matching shoes looked amazing.

I smiled at myself and said, *"Yea, though I walk through the valley of the shadow of death, I will fear no evil: for thou art with me; thy rod and thy staff they comfort me."*

Walking back over to my bed, I picked up my bible, which was my mother's. I ran my hand over the book and smiled as I thought of her. The Bible looked beat up, but it was comforting to me. I knew my mother's hands touched every single page of this bible hundreds of times and it made me feel like she was near. I missed her so much.

There was a light tap on my door. I looked up to see my son Aden standing there looking handsome as ever in his gray suit. I didn't hear him come in.

"Are you ready, mom?" he asked.

Some of the bruises on his face finally were beginning to disappear. He was looking like his old self again even though his demeanor was still one of pain and resentment.

"I sure am," I said walking to him.

"You look beautiful."

"Thank you, son. You look debonair yourself."

"Well you know how I do," he said popping his collar.

I giggled.

"You sure you want to do this today?" he asked for reassurance.

"I prayed about everything and even though my stomach is a little nervous, I know I got this," I said confidently.

Not wanting to enquire but feeling like I needed to, I asked, "Have you spoken to your father, Aden?"

His body tightened at the mention of his dad. The two of them still weren't doing well. I'd talked with Aden and told him in order for him to move on with his life, he needed to let go of this bitterness. It wasn't healthy for him. As much as he claimed he was okay, I knew he wasn't. Because if he was, he could look his father in the face and be okay with the man that stood before him, regardless of his indiscretions. Hate was a powerful thing that could take over your life and affect you in ways you couldn't imagine.

Seeing my son's hesitation I began to speak.

"Aden, honey, you have to let go and let God. I've told you this before."

"It's going to take some time, mom."

"I know. We are only human. But don't let the actions of others stop your soul from going to heaven."

Aden smiled kindly and said, "I understand mom."

Patting him gently on his cheek, I tucked my purse under my arm, cupped my mother's bible in the other and said, "It's about that time. We need to get to the church."

Juliana

I watched Aden escort his mother into the church. The two of them were all smiles as the hugged and greeted Payton, Elaine, and Diego, who stood waiting for them in the vestibule. A big happy family reunion it was. But Carson was nowhere to be found. His car was in his pastor's parking space near the back, but I hadn't seen him. The fact he arrived separate from his family let me know he was indeed on the outs with them and this made me happy.

I tried to enter the church, but some deacons were waiting at the door letting me know I couldn't come into the sanctuary. Since when did they start rejecting people who wanted to come to God's house. I wasn't the one who caused the altercation that happened. That was the First Lady. Yet, they allowed her to walk up in there like she was a queen. I was sick of her. What did she have that I didn't? Why was it everyone loved her, and I seemed to be shunned at every turn? I went to the grocery store and saw some members who moved away from me like I had something. I saw some others at the hair salon and they leaned into each other whispering and

pointing in my direction giving me dirty looks. I wasn't
the married one, Carson was. He chose me and as soon
as everybody understood what we had was real, the
easier it would be for them to accept me as the next First
Lady of this church.

The parking lot was full to capacity. People were
parking down the street to get up in here tonight. I
couldn't understand this. Either the members were very
forgiving, or they were just noisy and wanted to see what
was going to happen tonight. Word in the street was
Amelia was speaking to the congregation. To be a fly on
that wall would be priceless. I knew if I was in the
congregation, I would have had tomatoes to throw at her
behind. I would boo her to get off the pulpit, so my man
could preach.

Carson didn't know how much I loved him.
Tonight, he would understand and by the end of the
service, he was going to be walking arm and arm with me
out of that building.

I saw Aden hold up a finger. He said something
and walked back out the church, reaching in his pocket.
He must've forgot something. His family entered the
church and the deacons guarding the doors closed them.

Aden pulled out his keys because I saw the blink
of the tail lights of his car. He parked in his mother's
parking space which happen to be very convenient for
what I wanted to do. I wasn't sure why he was going
back to his car, but I figured this was my chance to

finally speak to him since he hadn't returned any of my calls.

He was reaching over in the passenger seat for something when I spoke.

"Hi Aden."

When he stood, he was holding a tattered bible in his hands. Scowling at me, he slammed the car door closed and started to walk away.

"Aden, say something."

"How dare you show your face here tonight after what you've done," he seethed.

"I wanted to see you."

He whirled around. His eyes were hollow with madness.

"You've seen me. Now leave."

"Please, talk to me Aden. I've called you several times, but you keep ignoring me."

"For good reason. The first being you sleeping with my father. The second being the fact you used me to get to him. And third, but definitely not least, you hurt my mother. You are a homewrecker; Juliana and I will never forgive you or my father for what you have done to us."

"Aden, I'm sorry. I really am," I apologized.

"Save your apologies," he said angrily.

"I couldn't choose. I liked you and him. I never meant to hurt you."

"How sick are you? Did you really think I would be okay being with my father's side piece?" he asked frowning.

"I was more to Carson than just a side piece."

"Mistress, side piece, I'm being nice. I can think of a few other choice names you are but I'm trying to be a gentlemen."

"You enjoyed being with me, Aden, and I was with you because I wanted to be."

Crossing his arms, he asked, "So let's hear it, Juliana. Was I better than my dad or did he rock your world better than I did?"

"You were better, of course," I lied.

He nodded chuckling deviously. The laughter of some church members entering the church caused the both of us to look in that direction. I could hear the sound of church music playing which meant I knew he had to get inside.

"I indulged you for a bit but now I'm done. Don't call me. Don't approach me. Act like I never existed. As far as I'm concerned, you are dead to me."

Aden turned and started walking back to the churches entrance.

Reaching in my back pocket, I pulled out the weapon I had. Running up behind Aden, I plunged the knife into his back. His scream caught in his throat as the blade ripped into his flesh causing him to stumble. I withdrew the knife. Unsteadily, he turned to me, eyes big as saucers. I plunged it into him again. This time he fell to his knees. The bible he was holding tumbled to the ground. He tried to say something but nothing but labored breaths came from him. Falling to the ground, he looked up at me with eyes filled with desperation. Straddling him, I lowered myself down on him with my eyes still transfixed on his.

"You didn't expect this, huh, Aden. I can tell from the bugged eyed expression you have on your face. I was really hoping things were going to turn out different between us, but you didn't go along with the plan. All you had to do was love me enough to get me closer to your father. That was all but you couldn't even do that for me."

Aden said nothing as he struggled to breath.

"Don't worry. I'll go to your dad and see if he'll give me another chance. If he doesn't comply, I guess he's going to suffer the same fate as you. It was nice knowing you," I said tapping him on the cheek and rising to my feet to go get my man.

Amelia

I was grateful to receive a warm welcome from the members of the church. Many came to me, hugging me, kissing me on the cheek and telling me I was in their prayers. Here I was thinking they would label me as a fraudulent person, but many knew that was not in my character and that made me feel wonderful. My mother's words resonated within me.

"If people don't remember anything else about you, the one thing they will remember is your character. So give the best of you at all time." I smiled at her words of wisdom.

I sat in my usually spot in the pew with my family sitting by my side. There was a guest choir who came with the visiting minster and they were tearing the church up with their sounds. I stood a couple of times getting filled up with the spirit. The church was on fire and you could feel Jesus was definitely in the building tonight.

When I went to sit down from getting my praise on, I felt a soft hand on my shoulder and looked to see it was Skye. She smiled at me. I stood and embraced her lovingly. We hadn't talked since that night everything happened, but I was so glad to see her here. I stepped out, allowing her to maneuver in the space next to me. She kissed Payton on the cheek and smiled at the rest of the family on the pew. And that's when I realized Aden wasn't back yet. I forgot my mother's bible in the car and he went back to get it for me. I got so caught up in the spirit that I didn't notice my own son wasn't sitting with us.

I leaned over and whispered, "Did you see Aden when you came in?"

Skye shook her head. I immediately became concerned as an unsettled feeling fell over me. I looked to the side to see Carson sitting on the front pew to my right, where the deacons usually sat. I heard he removed himself from the pulpit after everything that happened but the fact he was man enough to show his face up in the church gave him some credit in my eyes even though he sat alone. I felt sorry for him in that moment.

I wasn't sure how everyone was treating him, and I knew I shouldn't care but a small part of me did. The only thing I could do was pray for him, our family and for Greater Faith Baptist Church.

Mother Betty approach the podium and I knew it was time for me to go up. She was the only one I wanted introducing me because I knew she loved me and my family.

"Praise the Lord, church," she greeted. "We have someone who would like to speak to you tonight. When she called and asked me if I could introduce her, I immediately said yes. Some of you may not want to hear from her but I know most of you need to hear from her," Mother Betty said.

Skye reached over and gripped my hand and I looked at her with a smile.

"I love her and her family dearly. Church, please join me as we welcome our first Lady, Sister Amelia Reid."

I stood, approaching the podium where Mother Betty was trying my best not to trip or fall as nervousness settled in. My legs felt like spaghetti noodles. I embraced Mother Betty who lovingly kissed me on the cheek before returning to her seat. Once I turned to face the congregation, I was stunned to see the entire church standing to their feet. I became choked up as I looked into the faces of my family smiling back at me.

Elaine, with her crazy self, threw two thumbs up mouthing, "You got this."

I nodded at her and took in the love the church was giving me. Tears began to well up in my eyes as I felt the spirit of God fill me.

"Thank you. Thank you so much church," I struggled to say.

When I said that, it sounded like the claps got louder. I lifted my hands up to the sky thanking God for his mercy and his grace. The spirit hit me, and I began praise dancing right there at the podium. The pianist began to play, and the church erupted in praise. I don't know how long that went on but when I calmed myself to step back up to the podium all I could do was scream, "Yes. Yes. Yes Jesus, Hallelujah," over and over again.

"Thank you, Jesus. He is worthy. He is worthy. I said he is worthy, to be praised, amen," I pointed to the ceiling.

"Yes," rang out and finally the church began to calm enough for me to speak.

"Giving all honor and glory to my Lord and Savior Jesus Christ, to our guest minister of the night who traveled a mighty long way to be here, his magnificent choir, to the visiting ministers, my family, to the deacons and deaconess. And last but certainly not least to you the congregation, Good evening."

Everyone greeted me back.

"I was a little nervous to speak to you all tonight, but I knew I had to if it wasn't but to say I'm sorry," I paused. "I'm sorry for my actions in this sanctuary the other night. There was no excuse for it. I never should have allowed the devil to get the best of me. I never should have touched that woman. As they say I should have turned the other cheek. I disrespected God's house.

I disrespected you all, and I disrespected myself," I said holding my hands out to my side.

"Amen," a few said.

"I'm not perfect. I'm human and I make mistakes. I don't claim to be the best Christian. I don't try to think I'm better than anybody else. And I don't ever want to forget where I came from. I joke with my family all the time that there is First Lady Amelia Reid. Then there is Amelia Reid who is still working on being the best she can be. *Steve Harvey* said it best, God's not through with me yet."

"Yes," someone shouted.

"I was a woman hurt. I was stunned, angry, devastated, embarrassed, and ashamed by everything that I found out and everything that happened," I said glancing Carson's way. He was watching intently just like everyone else. "I took the position as First Lady seriously. I tried anyway. Granted, I've failed in some areas. I can admit that. I know I may fail again because again, I'm not perfect," I paused. "You don't have to forgive me because the only forgiveness I'm seeking is from my father," I said pointing to the ceiling. "I've ask for forgiveness tenfold and I know if I continue to rely on him, even during this storm in my life right now, I'm going to be okay."

A clap rang out loud, but it sounded like it came from one person. As I scanned the crowded sanctuary, I

326

noticed a woman walking down the aisle. To my utter dismay, it was Juliana.

"Bravo, Amelia. Bravo," she yelled, making her way to the front of the church.

Grumbles filled the church as everyone watched in horror as Juliana came stepping before me in a pair of dark denim jeans, a pink tee, and a gun which was tucked in the front waistband of her jeans. You would think the church was talking about her and the gun she yielded but what everybody was really grumbling about was the fact her pink tee was covered in something red.

Immediately Aden popped into my head and I knew the crimson tint all over her tee belonged to my son.

Amelia

I couldn't move, nor could I say anything. All I could do was watch as Juliana made her way closer to the front of the church. A couple of Deacons started to rush her, but she reached into her waistband and pull out the gun causing them to halt. Church members began to scream, and chaos erupted. Many jumped to their feet hustling to get themselves out of the sanctuary. It was utter mayhem. But not everybody left. The visiting minister stayed in his placed along with my family which included Skye who hadn't budged either. A few church members decided to take their chances and watch how this was going to unfold. I looked to my left to see Carson too hadn't budged as he gazed at me with fear embedded on his face. Our moment of connecting, we both knew something had happened to our son.

He got up and boldly approached Juliana who had the gun pointed at the Deacons who tried to rush her.

When she saw him get up, she turned the weapon on him. He held his hands up in defense letting her know he didn't want any trouble. He got up the nerve to ask what I wanted to know but was too afraid ask. The words were caught in my throat. Plus, I was afraid of what her answer would be.

"Juliana, what have you done to our son?" Carson asked grimly.

"Oh, you mean, Aden? He's outside," she said like she was talking about a good friend. Her demeanor was laid back, like this was normal for her.

"Outside where?" he questioned.

One of the deacons got up slowly and was behind Juliana. He gave Carson a knowing look like he was going to check to see if he saw our son. I moved from around the podium and started to bolt down the other aisle. I was going outside to search for my son.

"Don't you move," Juliana warned.

I ignored her, attempting to make my way down the aisle but a gunshot rang out. Screams were heard, and I halted, afraid to turn around to see if that bullet was in someone.

"Get back over here," she demanded.

I turned around slowly, to see her arm in the air. Luckily, the round she fired went into the ceiling.

"What did you do to my son?" I asked angrily.

"Didn't I say get over here?" she waved the gun for me to move closer to Carson.

"I swear if you hurt him…."

"You are not going to do anything!" she said through clenched teeth.

Carson interrupted and said, "Is that blood on your clothes?"

She looked down at her shirt like she hadn't noticed.

"Wow. I didn't know I had this one me. I guess when I plunged that knife in him, that's when his blood got on me."

"No," I cried in agony losing my battle to hold myself up as I crumpled to the floor.

I could hear Payton crying which was surprising over my own weeping for my son.

"Awh. Poor Amelia. It's okay. You will see him soon, don't you worry your pretty little head about it," she taunted.

I cried uncontrollably wondering was my son okay or was it already too late because she'd killed him.

Carson got choked up himself as he tried to clear his trembling voice.

"This was between me and you, Juliana. You didn't have to involve my family," Carson admonished.

"Your family is the reason we are not together," Juliana erupted.

"If it's me you want, then take me. Leave these innocent people alone and let's leave here right now together," he coaxed.

Juliana's eyes softened as she looked hopeful at Carson.

"You really mean that?" she asked.

"Yes I do. I love you. I had to tell you I didn't until all of this died down. You know I had to go before the church trustees this evening about what happened."

"No, I didn't know, baby."

"Yes, that's why I'm here. Then there could be possible charges filed against me. That's why I couldn't come be with you right away," Carson explained.

Pointing at Juliana, I said, "She killed our son, Carson. How could even want to be with her?"

Juliana turned her gun on me yelling, "Don't talk to him like that."

"Wait, Juliana. I got this," Carson said.

Juliana's hand trembled like she was trying to maintain not pulling the trigger on me. Carson stepped in front of the gun and turned to face me.

"Amelia, I've doubted for years he was even my son."

His words cut me to the core. Was he really serious? I looked into his eyes, but I honestly couldn't tell whether he meant what he was saying or if this was a trick to get Juliana away from here. I struggled to my feet and approached my husband. Once I was right up on him, I reached out and smack the crap out of him.

"Hey, don't you put your hands on my man like that," Juliana said, stepping closer as she pointed the gun at me. Carson held his hand up for her to stop, and she did.

"Amelia, I haven't loved you for a long time. Juliana is who I want to be with. I just didn't know how to tell you."

"I'm going to kill you," my brother Diego bolted up in anger. Elaine grabbed his arm for him to sit down, not wanting him to get harmed in anyway.

"I'm sorry, Diego, but the truth is the truth," Carson told him. Turning back to me, he said, "I hope you can understand this."

"The two of you deserve each other," I spat.

I could hear sirens in the distance and was grateful someone had called the police. Juliana looked back like the law was getting ready to burst through the church doors at any moment.

"Juliana, we have to get out of here. The cops will be here any minute," Carson begged.

"You're right," she said fearfully.

Carson approached her and gently cupped her face in the palms of his hands. He ignored the weapon she was holding, which was still pointed in my direction.

I looked at my daughter, Elaine, Diego, and Skye who sat there watching. None of them looked afraid. The only thing I was afraid of was my son being seriously hurt. If anything happened to Aden, I would blame Carson. If it wasn't for him getting involved with this woman, none of this would be happening now.

Juliana leaned in and kissed Carson. He received her without flinching. I was disgusted by their affection.

Breaking their connection, Carson said, "Let's leave out the back," he gestured, heading in the direction of his office.

Juliana nodded, lowering her weapon happily. Carson took her by the hand and began leading her away from us.

"We really are doing this?" she said happily.

Null and Void

"Yes honey, we are."

"You love me?" she questioned.

"Yes," he answered.

"So you don't mind if I do this?"

Juliana lifted her weapon and pointed it back at me.

My brother Diego yelled, "No."

I looked at her with no fear in my heart. If it was my time to go, then so be it and that's when I heard the sound of the gun being fired.

Skye

The First Lady was on the floor of the church, blood oozing from her midsection. I sat there, not able to move. Elaine and Diego scurried towards her. She wasn't moving. Payton was rocking back and forth crying hysterically and screaming to the top of her lungs as we watched Amelia bleed out onto the carpet floor.

Her mint colored suit was quickly turning crimson as the colored expanded. Diego crouched down beside her and called out to her, but she wasn't responding. He tore his jacket off, and then his shirt, balling it up to apply pressure to her wound.

"We have to stop the bleeding," he stammered.

Elaine was at her head, caressing her face talking to her, telling her, "Don't you leave us. You fight, Amelia. You hear me. You fight."

Carson began yelling at Juliana who was trying to pull him out the back, but he kept standing there screaming, "I'm sorry, Amelia. Honey, I'm sorry."

The look in his eyes was one of hurt as he watched his wife's lifeless body lay at the altar of the church.

"What did you do?" he yelled. "Why did you do that?" he asked Juliana.

"She doesn't mean anything to you anymore."

"But she was my wife."

"I'm going to be your new wife. Now let's go before the cops come in here," she urged.

Carson looked around like he didn't know what to do. Our eyes connected for a moment as a tear streamed down his face. Juliana tugged at his arm to pull him and he hesitantly went with her finally leaving Amelia to bleed out on the church floor.

It seemed like it took forever for the paramedics to arrive. They rushed in and dropped down beside Amelia to see where the bullet penetrated her. It entered the side opposite her heart. I considered that to be a good thing. I closed my eyes and started praying to God to save her, to allow her to live for her children. We needed her. I needed her. There was no way God was done with her. She had too much work on this earth to do. It wasn't time for her to go.

"She has a pulse," one of the paramedics blurted.

They hurriedly lifted her to the stretcher and rushed Amelia out of the church with Diego and Elaine closely behind them.

I stood looking over at Payton who'd checked out. She was staring straight ahead. I wondered where her fiancé was. Why wasn't he here supporting her?

Going over to her, I lifted her by her arm. For the first time in minutes, she looked at me.

"Is my mother going to be okay?" she asked barely over a whisper.

"Yes," I said, hoping my words would be true. "Come on Payton," I pulled her into my arms. Tears were steadily streaming down her cheeks, but she wasn't as hysterical as she was a moment ago. That was until we got outside. Once she saw two sets of ambulances and one of them loading Aden into one of them, Payton lost it again.

"Noooooooooo" Payton wailed, falling to her knees as the pressure of tonight's events sent her over the edge.

"Can I get some help over here?" I demanded.

A paramedic approached, and I asked, "Please, can you give her something to calm her?"

A commotion broke out as some police officers were trying to prevent Diego from getting in the ambulance with his sister. His massive frame, undoubtedly, was threatening. I hoped it wouldn't be a situation where the cops would shoot an unarmed black man all because he wanted to be by his sibling's side. Luckily the paramedics gestured for Diego to enter and the officers released him to jump in the ambulance to be by his sister's side.

Payton trembled and screamed as both ambulances jetted out of the parking lot to get Amelia and Aden to the hospital for treatment.

The paramedic helping me gestured for help from a third ambulance that approached.

Elaine came over to me and asked, "Can you stay with Payton?"

"Yes. Go ahead. I know you want to get to the hospital. Go. I got her," I said urgently and watched as Elaine ran to her vehicle and speed out hurriedly.

Payton began to hyperventilate. One of the paramedics reached inside his bag and pulled out a paper bag. He placed it over her mouth telling her to breathe.

She struggled at first but moments later her breathing became steady. The paramedic stuck a needle into her arm to sedate her. It worked almost immediately. He removed the bag, and said, "I think it's best if we take her to the hospital as well."

I nodded in agreement and watched as they carted her off into the third ambulance.

Wanting to get to the hospital myself, I rushed to my car. Fumbling to get my keys out, I dropped them. When I reached down to pick them up, a hand swooped in and grabbed them for me. When I looked up, I saw it was Dante.

I never been so happy to see anyone in my life. Without thinking, I wrapped my arms around his neck and hugged him tightly. Tears began to spill from me as tonight's events settled in.

"I got you," he whispered.

I didn't want to let him go. I felt like I couldn't. He was my comfort in this moment of trouble and seemed to be here for me always at the right time.

Finally letting go of him, I swiped at my tears and began to speak but he knew what I was going to say.

"I was here tonight with mom. I saw part of what happened. Once that woman walked in with that gun, I had to get my mother to safety."

I nodded, understanding completely.

"One of her friends has taken her home. As bad as she didn't want me to stay, I told her I had to be here for a good friend of mine."

I smiled.

"I'll drive you to the hospital, if that's okay."

I nodding knowing it wasn't a good idea to drive myself. As Dante walked me around to the passenger side of my car, a gun shot rang out, causing the entire parking lot to duck to safety. We both huddled next to the car. I heard the police scream the shot came from inside the church. Pastor Reid and Juliana were in the church. I'd already witness way more than I wanted to, and I didn't want to see who else could be a victim to that gunshot. I was ready to get to the hospital to find out how Aden and Amelia were doing, and I was happy Dante was the one by my side.

Juliana

I looked across the office at Carson who stood glaring at me with a smoking gun in his hand. I couldn't believe it. He'd actually shot me. I looked down at my pink tee becoming crimson with my own blood spewing from me. It took my body moments to realize I was hit. Fortunately, I didn't feel any pain. I didn't know if it was my body protecting itself or if it was actual shock of not believing the man I loved put a bullet in me.

He walked over to me and looked down at my wounded body.

"Why?" I asked him.

"Did you really think I was going anywhere with you after what you did to me and my family?"

"But…"

"You have ruined my life and I thought it was fitting that I ruined yours," he said coldly.

This angered me. I looked around for my weapon which fell out my hand when I collapsed to the floor. It

341

was inches from my grasped. Carson figured out what I was trying to do and he quickly kicked it away from me.

"Not today. You are not going to get off that easily."

"Oh, you thought I was going to kill myself."

He nodded.

"You would be right but that was after I put a bullet in your head," I told him.

"All you had to do was walk away when I told you we were over."

"I've walked away too many times. Men like you use women and then toss them away like their nothing."

"I never thought you were nothing, Juliana," he admitted with a hint of compassion.

"This was why I fell in love with you. You were different. And Aden is much like you," I told him. "Either of you would have been a great catch for me but I wanted you."

"I'm sorry for hurting you," he apologized. "But this ends today. I can't have you hurting my family anymore."

"So you are going to kill me?" I asked.

Before he had a chance to answer, the door to Carson's office burst open and the police stood with their weapons drawn. Instantly they pointed them at Carson who immediately lifted his hands in the air.

"Put your weapon down," an officer yelled.

"He tried to kill me," I screamed, acting like I feared for my life. "He shot his wife and tried to kill his son. And now he wants to kill me."

Carson glowered at me. I wished the officers would pull the trigger on him.

"Get down on the ground," they demanded.

Carson obeyed each request and the next thing I knew, they were walking him out in handcuffs.

"Why? Why did he do this?" I asked as the paramedics began working on me. Once I was on the stretcher and they were wheeling me outside to the awaiting ambulance, an officer approached the gurney.

Handcuffs were slapped on my right wrist and the other end attached to the gurney.

"What are you doing?" I asked in confusion.

"Juliana Simmons, you are under arrest for the attempted murder of Amelia Reid and Aden Reid."

"But—"

"You have the right to remain silent. Anything you say can and will be used against you in the court of law," he continued, ignoring me, as he read me my rights.

Skye

When I finally walked into my house, I kicked my heels off and walked straight to my sofa collapsing from exhaustion.

"I'm so tired," I said to Dante who was closing the door behind himself.

"It has been a long night," he said.

"And a crazy one," I threw my feet up on the sofa and stretched out. "I still can't believe everything that happened."

Dante came over and sat on the other end of the sofa, since I practically took up the majority of it. He reached over and grabbed one of my feet and began pressing into the bottom massaging it. I swear I had died and gone to heaven.

"That feels so good," I moaned.

When he applied more pressure to the center of my foot, I felt a slight tingle between my thighs. I wanted to jerk my foot away, but this massage was feeling so good, I couldn't bring myself to do that.

"I'm glad your friend and her son are going to be okay," Dante said bringing me out of the daze I was in. I felt like I could drift off to sleep but I tried my best to stay up so I could enjoy this foot massage.

"It was nothing but God," I declared.

Dante was by my side the entire night and we didn't leave until this morning when we knew Amelia and Aden were going to be okay. They would be in the hospital for a few days. Aden had the most life threatening injuries and if it wasn't for a member who saw him on the ground, who happened to be nurse to work on him, he may not have made it. God was still in charge. Prayers did work. We may not understand why things happen but it's a rhyme and a reason why things come to pass the way they do. It may not be a lesson for me, but it could be a lesson for someone else.

"I don't think the hospital has ever seen so many people waiting to see how a patient was doing."

Giggling, I said, "I know right. We brought the church to the hospital. We practically had a service right there in the waiting room."

"Where one or two or gather?"

"One of two hundred," I giggled again. "When the doctor finally came out, it looked like everybody stood to find out how they were doing. As much praying as I have been doing, my faith wavered."

"Why do you say that?" Dante asked.

"One reason was because of what happened in my marriage or what I thought was a marriage. I got cheated on just like Mrs. Reid did but the outcome was different. To witness her get shot and later hear about Aden, it made you wonder why things like this were allowed to happen to individuals who loved God."

"One thing is for certain, we are not free of bad things happening because we worship God. If everything was fine all the time, then why would we ever need to go to God for anything?"

"You sure know a lot about God for someone who doesn't go to church much."

"I have a praying mother he kept me in church when I was younger. I don't go as much as I should, but it doesn't mean I don't know God for myself."

I nodded, still enjoying the relief he was bringing to my tired feet.

"Thank you for being by my side, Dante. I don't know where you came from but I'm so glad you showed up."

"Any excuse to be around you is a good one."

A moment fell between us as our eyes locked. I smiled thinking how great this man was. As he pulled my other foot into his lap to start massaging it, there was a knock at my door.

Dante looked at me and asked, "Are you expecting anybody?"

I frowned and said, "No."

I removed my feet from Dante's lap and got up to see who was at the door.

"Why haven't you answered your phone? I have been worried sick about you," Seth said brushing pass me in a panic. He halted when he saw Dante rising from the sofa. He turned and gawked at me in anger.

"Oh, okay. I see why you didn't answer your phone. Here I am worried about you and what happened at the church and you cuddled up with this fool."

Dante bristled, like he was ready to pounce on Seth, but he maintained his composure.

"First of all, I didn't answer my phone because I was at the hospital all night long and my phone died while I was there."

"You home now. You should have plugged your phone up to call me," he stated.

"I don't answer to you anymore, Seth. I thought I was clear about that during our last conversation. We are not married and could go our separate ways."

"You decided that, not me."

"Oh really, and you sleeping with Fatima had nothing to do with our relationship falling apart?"

Seth stood dumbfounded.

"I appreciate you being concerned about me but I'm going to need you to leave so I can go back to enjoying my company. Make sure you tell Fatima I said hello," I said holding the door open for him to exit.

Seth always wanted me to stand up for myself and here I was doing just that. Too bad he was on the receiving end of it. Taking one last look at Dante, he exited my home.

Dante sat back down, and I walked over to the sofa reclaim my spot.

"He wants you back, you know," Dante told me.

"I know," I said looking into his handsome face. "But I meant what I said. I'm done with him. I've moved on."

"I'm happy to hear that."

"Are you now?"

"Only if you are considering moving on with me."

"Dante, are you trying to take advantage of a vulnerable woman?" I joked.

He smirked but shocked me when he got down on one knee. My heart rate quickened, not understand what this man was doing. He took my left hand into his and gazed at me lovingly.

"Skye, would you do me the honors and make me the happiest man ever?"

Amelia

Elaine was by my bedside when I woke up along with my brother Diego and my daughter Payton. When I went to move, a sharp pain shot through my side and I whence in agony.

"Don't move," my brother told me.

"Where am I?" I asked confused.

"You are in the hospital," Diego said.

"I'm so glad to see you are okay, mom," Payton added with tears streaming down her face.

And that's when it hit me. The memories of what happened came flooding back. Juliana pointing that gun at me and pulled the trigger. Then Aden came into my mind.

"Where is Aden?" I asked frantically trying to sit up, causing more pain to radiated throughout my body.

"He's fine, Amelia. Stop trying to get up," my brother told me.

"I don't believe you. You are telling me that, so I won't get upset," I began to cry.

"I wouldn't do that to you," he said.

"I want to see him. I want to see for myself my son is fine," I protested.

"Please, calm down. You will see him" Elaine chimed in gently rubbing my forehead.

"I want to see him, now," I demanded. "I want to lay my eyes on my son."

"Mom, I'm right here," I heard Aden's voice say.

Diego turned around to see Aden being wheeled in by a nurse. He too was in a hospital gown with a slight smile on his face. When I saw my son's face, it brought relief and joy to me.

"My baby," I called out, reaching out to him. I had to touch him to make sure it was really him. I prayed I wasn't dreaming or hallucinating because I didn't think I could handle if this was not my reality.

The nurse pushed Aden closer until he was able to take my hand into his. His warm hand filled my heart with more elation. I began to cry more.

"Are you okay?"

"Yes, mom, I'm fine."

"But I thought…"

"Don't say it. Your baby boy is good. Look at me. I'm still handsome as ever," he said chuckling causing everyone to do the same.

Tears streamed down the sides of my face as I thanked God for protecting my son and not taking him away from me.

"Has anyone seen dad?" Aden asked hesitantly.

All eyes darted as my brother began to speak.

"Carson is being held in jail."

"For what?" I asked.

"Shooting Juliana."

My brother explained everything he knew, and I felt so bad that I ever thought Carson would choose that woman over me. It wasn't hard to think this when he cheated on me with her. But he was trying to save us all, feeling like this entire event was his fault.

With a doleful expression, Aden began to speak.

"Lying on that ground after being stabbed by Juliana, all I could think about was all of you, including dad," he said getting choked up. "I didn't want to leave this earth with my father thinking I hated him."

I squeezed his hand, not able to rise like I wanted to.

"Sweetie, your father knows you do not hate him," I reassured him.

"I treated him so bad. I put my hands on him. What type of son does that?" he asked getting more upset.

"Despite what happened, Aden, what matters is the love is still here. Your father loves you and Payton, and he knows you love him too. Grace be the glory, God has given you a second chance to right whatever wrong you feel like you've done," I said.

"I prayed God would give me a second chance. Holding grandma's bible, I promised him if he let me live, I would resolve things with dad. And he's granted me my wish," he broke down.

I lovingly smiled at my son with my own tears flowing freely.

"God is so awesome. Even in the midst of this storm, he's still working things out, hallelujah," I shouted.

Elaine seconded that with her own hallelujah.

"You know what, I've had enough of this crying mess," she said jovially. "The first thing we are going to do is have a board game night or something to bring some fun back into this family."

"That sounds like an awesome plan to me," Payton agreed.

"When we get out of here, what would make me feel even better is if mom cooked my favorite meal," Aden hinted.

"Boy, what's wrong with you? Mom is injured and recovering like you are," Payton scolded him.

"I'm saying mom's food would be good right now. Did you see what they tried to feed us in this place? That food is what's going to kill us, much like yours Payton," Aden joked.

"Boy, you got problems," Elaine added.

His sister playfully hit her brother.

"Ouch, I'm recovering too," he told her.

"I can cook," Payton told him.

"If you say so but our previous dog Sparky would disagree, may he rest in peace," Aden said lowering his head for a moment of silence. "You stole what spark he had left."

The room erupted in laughter.

"Mom, will you tell him I can cook?"

"Leave your sister alone, Aden. You know she's learning," I added.

"Learning how to hurt somebody, mom. We all need to say a prayer for Rowan because he's doing to need it when he marries her."

"I feel sorry for the woman who decides to make Aden her man because she's going to have a problem on her hands," Diego chimed in.

"Why?" Aden asked.

"Because she's never going to be able to measure up to Amelia. A woman is going to have to be some kind of special for you to put her before Amelia. She's spoiled you rotten," my brother said.

"He's a mama's boy for sure," Payton added.

"Yes, I am, a proud one at that, just in case you didn't know."

Aden giggled along with the rest of the room. It felt good seeing my family all together and laughing with one another. The only person missing was Carson. I missed him so much. I didn't know what was going to happen with our marriage but right now the only thing I was going to dwell on was healing my family along with healing myself.

EPILOGUE

11 Months Later

Skye

"Million Dollar Question has become number one on the New York Times best seller's list, Skye. Congratulations on this accomplishment," the interviewer for *Ebony* magazines said.

"Thank you."

"You know this book got a lot of people stirred up. Instead of being posed with would you go outside your marriage and sleep with someone else for one million dollars, your book poses the question, if you found out your marriage was not legal, and the person was cheating on you, would you marry him for one million dollars?" the woman asked.

"Yes, because that's exactly what happened to me, minus the one million," I chuckled. "For me it was a million dollar question because this man, who I loved and who I thought was legally my husband, left me for his mistress. Finding out our marriage was a fraud made it easier for us to go our separate ways. Yet, this was the man I thought I was going to spend the rest of my life with."

"If your marriage was legal, would you have stayed with your husband?" she asked.

"I tried and looked like a complete idiot fighting for something that was not meant for me. My ex was a bump in my journey to get to the man God really wanted me to be with."

"So in actuality, your ex cheating lead you to the man you were truly meant to be with?" she asked.

"Absolutely."

"I see he's here with you today," she said flirtatiously gazing at Dante. "I hear you two are engaged to be married."

"We sure are? The wedding date is approaching us fast."

"In the book you mentioned how you saved yourself for your husband, who ended not being your true husband unfortunately, but I want to know are you doing the same with this handsome fellow?"

"Actually I am."

"Really?" she asked with surprise.

"If I don't think of myself as worthy of being waited for, then who would? Luckily Dante is the most patient and loving man I've ever laid my eyes on and I'm so thankful God saw fit to place him in my life."

She turned her attention to Dante and asked, "And you are okay with this because most men can't do a day without, you know, doing the do?"

"Skye is worth the wait," he said proudly.

"Girl, does he have any brothers?"

Laughing, I said, "He does, three of them."

"Are they single?"

"One is but he's with someone."

"Well if this is what the power of prayer can do for you, then I need to get on my knees tonight."

Some people chuckled.

"To pray, y'all. Get your minds out of the gutter," she winked at me.

My interview went on for another twenty minutes and then I was able to be on my merry way. Dante and I had a ceremony to attend and I didn't want to be late.

I was a happy woman and couldn't believe how much God had blessed me. Even though the devil tossed many obstacles my way, I ducked and dodged each of them knowing whatever I was going through, God was going to see me through.

This time last year I was a married woman but now I was in love with Dante. Seth called me for a while telling me how I was making a mistake by not giving us another chance. I heard things with him and Fatima weren't going great. If the rumors were true, it was because Fatima ended up cheating on him and was pregnant and she wasn't sure if the baby was the man she slept with or Seth's. Ironic right? Isn't that how it goes? You think what you have is not good until you get out there to see what you had was perfect. Unfortunately for Seth, I was done with him. I'd forgiven him. I had to in order for me to release that negativity and move on.

Dante reached over and grabbed my hand lovingly as he drove us to our destination.

"Did I tell you how beautiful you look?" he asked, checking me out.

"Thank you, Dante. But you do know you need to keep your eyes on the road and not on me right?" I said giggling.

I gawked at the two caret diamond Dante placed on my finger three months ago and I smiled warmly.

"Are you happy babe?" Dante asked drawing me out of my thoughts.

"Why do you ask?"

"I just wanted to know. I got to make sure you are good with how our life is going thus far."

"I'm ecstatic, Dante. From day one, you have kept a smile on my face and I love you for that. What about you? Are you happy?"

"Hey, I asked you to marry me. The fact you said yes not only made me the happiest man ever, it made my mother the happiest woman ever because she thought I was never going to get married."

I laughed.

"She wanted us to go down to the justice of the peace and do it because she thought I was going to get cold feet."

"I hope you wouldn't do me like that. The interviewer said men had needs."

"I'm not going to cheat on you like Seth, Skye. I promise you that. As for my needs, I'm good. Like I said to that interviewer earlier, you are worth the wait. I love you too much to ever hurt you."

He always knew what to say to ease any doubt I had about us. One thing I prayed about was to not let the negative actions of Seth affect my relationship with Dante. All men didn't cheat. However, pain clouded things for me at times and here was Dante reassuring me of his dedication to me.

"I hope you are ready for this journey with me, Skye. First is the marriage and you know the next thing is going to be babies?"

"What?" I asked.

"Mama said she wants ten grandchildren."

"All from me?" I questioned.

"Maybe. Mama had six."

"Well babe, I might can give you at least three."

"That many," he joked, and I playfully swatted at him.

Pulling up to the church, the parking lot was already full. Dante cut the car off and turned to me.

"Thank you for agreeing to be my wife," he said dotingly.

"Thank you for choosing me to be your wife."

We both kissed and I thanked God once again for sending me a man who truly loved me for me.

Amelia

The wedding was wonderful and now all of our friends and family were on the dance floor getting their groove on to Earth, Wind, and Fire's song *Celebration* at the reception. As I danced with Aden, I looked over to capture Carson dancing with our daughter Payton who looked lovely as ever.

I turned to my son and said, "I like the young woman you are seeing."

My son smiled as he looked over at her sitting at a table grinning at us.

"She is wonderful, isn't she?"

"You did good son."

"That means a lot coming from you."

"Don't mess it up. I know how you are."

"I'm not mom, I promise. I really like her. And trust me, I've learned my lesson. I'm glad to you see how happy you are," Aden said looking at me adoringly.

"This feels great. It's like our lives are back on tract."

"It is," Aden added.

"It wasn't easy."

"Who you telling? Almost a year ago we both were in the hospital recouping from what that crazy woman did," Aden said not mentioning Juliana's name.

After she was convicted of attempted murder for me and Aden, my son vowed never to say her name again. As you can see he was keeping that vow. She ended up getting forty five years in prison for what she did to us. I wished she would have received life but forty five years would have to do. To say that trial was a grueling process was an understatement. She refused to plead guilty. She wanted her day in court and by law she deserved that. Little did most of us know Juliana used this opportunity to throw everyone under the bus? Here we were thinking only our dirty laundry was going to be on full display and in more detail this time, but she ended up giving the names of all the men she'd slept with. This woman had recorded videos of a lot of her affairs, including the one she had with Carson. Her trial was a media spectacle and she played the role as the leading actress in a drama serious. Juliana ate up every bit of the lime light. This woman even had the audacity to blackmail some of the men to try to help her get the charges dropped or else she would release the information. To the dismay of some men, that came out in trial as well with them paying a considerable amount financially, one of them being a top judge in our community. He had to stepped down from his position after getting caught trying to bribe someone.

The heftiest price being paid was that of many families being torn apart by this spectacle. Some of the same men who wanted to kick Carson out of our church, were witnesses in the trial with their own secrets being exposed, including Deacon Dwight. Carson didn't look so bad compared to everything else that came out. In the beginning, he was made to look like the evildoer, which he was because he never should have cheated and lied about who he was. But by the end of that trial, he definitely looked like the victim.

Carson came over and asked, "Aden, can I dance with Amelia, please?"

Aden paused. With a smile, he stepped to the side and said, "You sure can." Giving his father a hug, Aden went over to his sister as Carson stepped in front of me.

"Now you know you are not going to show me up Carson?" I said playfully.

"Well, you better get it in gear and join in because you know how I do."

The music changed and Gerald Levert's *Didn't We* stepping song started to play.

"You see. That's a sign," Carson quipped stepping close to me taking my hands into his. "Let's show these people how it's really done."

Carson and I began stepping. We turned, twirled, and spun with him even dipping me a few times. A crowd surrounded us and made us their main attraction. They hooped and hollered as we grooved like we'd never done before, and it felt great.

When the song was over, our friends and family cheered. Both of us bowed to them. I smiled and walked with him off the floor because I was truly tired after that show of dance moves. I wasn't young as I use to be, but I could still get my groove on even if it tired me out a lot faster.

A ding of a glass sounded, and we saw Aden standing and tapping his spoon against his champagne glass. The room grew quiet as everyone waited for him to speak.

"I'd like to make a toast to the bride and groom. We've been through so much over the past few months but as you can see, God has brought us all a mighty long way."

Claps rang out around us.

"This day is exactly the way it should be, with our family and our good friends coming together in love and unity."

"Here, here," my brother Diego said.

Aden held his glass up and said, "To the bride a groom. To my parents Benjamin Carson and Amelia Reid."

Claps rang out as people sipped their beverage. I leaned over and kissed my husband. I loved this man with every fiber of my being. Yes, I thought about kicking his behind to the curve and moving on with my life. But a whispered voice told me we all make mistakes. Not only did God let me know what needed to be done, he also showed me myself in this situation because I wasn't faultless by any means.

That's when I decided to give us a second chance. Yes, Carson wasn't forthcoming with me on a lot of things but the years of happiness and the life we'd built with one another out weighted everything. With our family on the brink of death, it opened up all of our eyes to what was important. I didn't know if we would work but I wouldn't know if I didn't at least give us another try.

Carson asked me to marry him again, under his real name, Benjamin. He legally had his middle name changed to Carson, this way we could still acknowledge him as that. BC was starting to become a nickname for him and he seemed to like it.

As happy as my husband was, I knew a part of him wished his sister Dee Dee was here. After her appearance at church that night, we hadn't seen, nor heard from her. The apartment he helped her get into, she moved out of and there was no signs of her. Despite what she'd done, Carson loved her. That was his sister and he cared for her deeply. Unfortunately, she didn't care about him. Regardless, we had to pray for her anyway.

As for the church, it was bad at first. Although the congregation accepted me, they were not too forgiving of Carson and what he'd done, which was to be expected. Still, it was our church, one we built from the ground up. No one could say he was not an excellent deliverer of the word. Preaching was something Carson loved to do. Right now he had a minister standing in for him. We didn't want to lose the members who wanted to continue to support us and the minister he got to serve in his place temporarily was amazing. Carson was going to school to get his real licensed to be a pastor. He'd already gotten his license to officiate weddings. Surprisingly he'd done six weddings in the last three months. A couple of lawsuits were filed against him by people he'd married but we settled that out of court. As for him shooting Juliana, the court considered it self-defense and no charges were filed against Carson. Miraculously, no charges were filed for his fraud as well. That too was settled with the courts and right now my husband was truly a free man.

Our relationship could have been a null and void situation, but I chose my husband and my family. Today was our wedding day, a fresh start to continue our lives together. There were hills and valleys, but I was thankful in the end I was blessed with the family and friends God surrounded me with.

"That's our song, honey," Carson said smiling as Luther Vandross' *Here and Now* played.

Carson stood and held out his hand for me to accompany him. I took it and we went back out to the dance floor as Mr. and Mrs. Benjamin Carson Reid.

Acknowledgments

First and foremost, I have to give all the honor and the glory to our Lord and Savior. I'm nothing without him.

This is a book I never thought I would be capable of writing. Me, a Christian book writer. But God, is all I can say. This book was placed in my spirit almost five years ago. I was hesitant to write it because it wasn't my genre but a friend of mine, Sonia Gravely told me to do it anyway. So I did.   This is my sixth published book. I love every last one of them but this one means so much more because of what it represents. It represents change, growth, maturing, belief, and faith. Much like my very first book, I cried when this one came out because it was a validation for me. I did something I never thought I would or could do. So, never say never.

I need to thank my husband, Wil. I love you so much. So many nights I've been in bed next to you with the lights off, you sleeping and my fingers tapping away with my writing. And you have been patient and compassionate knowing the love I have for my writing. Thank you for supporting me, baby.

I want to thank my children. My son's checks on me when I'm writing to see if I need anything or looks over my shoulder to see what I'm writing with this book, I could let him read it. LOL. I thank my daughters because they did read this book and told me loved it. You don't understand. My children haven't read my books for obvious reasons if you've been a supporter. This book was actually one they enjoyed reading because of what the book *didn't* contain. They don't like their mother being so explicit. I understand. I would feel some kind of way if my mother was explicit as well.

I want to thank my parents, Clarence and Rebecca. They are undoubtedly my rock and the best parents anyone can have. Anything I need, they are there. I thank God for them all the time and truly know how blessed I am to still have them in my life.

I want to thank Sonia Gravely for pushing me to write book that was placed in my spirit, to Denise (D.A.) Kelley for telling me it was time for me to expand my horizon and put this book out and for leading me to another awesome woman, Denora Boone, CEO of Anointed Inspirations Publishing (AIP). Thank you for giving me this opportunity. You just don't know how much I appreciate this. I hope I make you proud. To Ms. Patricia Liggon for telling me so many years ago to write until God changes it because he knows my heart. I battled for years with my style of writing feeling as thought it was wrong, but she told me no, to write how I write, which is what I did. She said when I changed and grew with time, so would my writing. Look at me now. I also want to thank Ms. Wanda Hester and Rochelle Cicero. These two ladies have read almost, if not all, of the books I've written. Besides my mother, they are the ones I go to first before making a decision on whether to publish. They have been supporters of me before my books and are my sounding boards. I value their opinion tremendously. I also have to thank the Anointed Inspirations Publishing (AIP) family. This group of individuals are absolutely astonishing. Our conversations are amazing. They have been so supportive welcoming me and making me feel like I've known them for years. What I love is we support one another. We cheer for one another. We pray for one another and those are the types of individuals you want to surround yourself around.

Last but not least I want to thank my family, friends, book clubs, book sellers, and book readers during my journey. I wish I can name all of you but I know I would forget some, which is never my intention. Thank you for always supporting me. I truly appreciate it. I know I may say this a lot, but I mean it. The best form of appreciation is to say thank you. Thank you!

Having faith in yourself is necessary to move forward with any dream you have within you. Nothing is impossible even though it feels that way many times over. I have more things I want to accomplish and I'm coming to a place in my life where I'm believing it's going to happen. God is real, and he continues to show me favor and prove to me he is indeed in the midst. He continues to bless me in so many ways even though at times I feel undeserving of his blessings. Remember, nothing is too hard for God. Keep your head up. Keep pushing forward. Don't give up. A mustard seed of faith. That's all you need. Remember that. God bless!

My favorite scripture. *"I can do all things through Christ who Strengthens me."* Philippians 4:13

CPSIA information can be obtained
at www.ICGtesting.com
Printed in the USA
LVOW13s1628220518
578094LV00009B/588/P